NOTHING EVER HAPPENS HERE

NOTHING EVER HAPPENS HERE

SARAH HAGGER-HOLT

YELLOW JACKET

In memory of my dad, who instilled in me
a love of language, storytelling, and
classic Broadway musicals

 YELLOW JACKET

An imprint of Little Bee Books
New York, NY
Text copyright © 2020 by Sarah Hagger-Holt
All rights reserved, including the right of
reproduction in whole or in part in any form.
Yellow Jacket and associated colophon
are trademarks of Little Bee Books.

Manufactured in China RRD 0121
Originally published in Great Britain
in 2020 by Usborne Publishing Ltd.
First U.S. Edition 2021
10 9 8 7 6 5 4 3 2 1
Library of Congress Cataloging-in-Publication Data
is available upon request.
ISBN 978-1-4998-1181-0
yellowjacketreads.com

For information about special discounts on
bulk purchases, please contact Little Bee Books at
sales@littlebeebooks.com.

The Beginning

This is Littlehaven. Nothing ever happens here.

No one famous was born here. Or lived here. Or even died here.

The main street has the same shops as every other main street in every other town.

Even when you walk and walk right to the edge of Littlehaven, there aren't rolling hills or mysterious woods, there are just flat fields, going off into the distance.

The most famous thing that happened here was hundreds of years ago. Someone, I can't remember who, invented a machine that halved the time you could harvest wheat or something. We went to see it on a trip in grammar school. All metal spikes and crushing wheels.

This is Littlehaven. Nothing ever happens here.

Until the spotlight hits my family . . .

Chapter One

On my bedside table, the clock flashes 3:00 am. I'm awake. I don't know what's woken me up, but now that I'm awake, I'm hungry.

Mom always moans about the amount I eat: another jar of peanut butter scraped clean, another box of Cheerios gone, another loaf of bread with only the crusts left at the bottom of the bag.

"I don't know where you put it all," she says. "Leave something for the rest of us, Izzy."

But Dad says, "Give her a break, Kath, she's just growing, aren't you, Izzy? Everyone's got to grow." And he crouches down to pretend he's smaller than me and that I'm a giant towering above him.

Sometimes, I like it. Sometimes, it's just embarrassing.

I lie there for a bit, thinking perhaps I'll go back to sleep. 3:04. 3:05. No, definitely hungry.

I pull on my pink robe and quietly head downstairs, thinking there might be some Rice Krispies left. Past Megan's room. Past Jamie's, with its tatty *Thomas the Train* poster still hanging on the door. Past Mom and Dad's.

I'm halfway down the stairs before I hear something. It's a kind of snuffling sound and a gasping sound and a hiccupping sound. It's so odd that I stop where I am to listen more closely.

Then I realize, it's someone crying. Not just a little bit. It's the sort of crying that stops you breathing properly, that leaves you all snotty and headachy and swollen-eyed.

There's light coming from under the living room door. I can hear Mom's voice murmuring softly, but not what she's saying.

The crying continues.

It's Dad.

Of course I've seen Dad cry before. He sniffs all the way through *The Wizard of Oz* and *Marley and Me*, welling up long before the dog dies. But nothing like this.

My stomach turns in on itself. I'm not hungry anymore.

I head back to my room and curl up tight under my

duvet, thinking of something, anything, to try and get the sound of Dad crying out of my head; my twelve times table, the names of all the children in *The Sound of Music* in order, what I'm going to wear tomorrow on the first day of the summer break. The numbers on the clock blinking past: 3:07. 3:08.

Chapter Two

"Jamie, come on, how long does it take to choose between Corn Flakes and Rice Krispies? Pass the box over." Jamie's in rapt concentration, staring at the cereal boxes in front of him.

"I'm doing the puzzle. There are only two words left to find."

"Pass them over. Come on. It's nearly time to go. I don't want to be late on the first day of school," I snap, pouring juice with one hand and trying to force my new black shoes on with the other. "Grace'll be here in a minute."

"Isabel, leave your little brother alone," says Mom. She looks me up and down. "Where's your tie?"

"In my pocket," I say with my mouth full of cereal, rolling out the green-and-blue striped St. Mary's tie to show her. "I don't want to put it on till I've eaten my breakfast, so it doesn't get milky."

Megan clatters down the stairs, skirt rolled up, black makeup visible around her eyes. "Where's my portfolio? Which of you has taken it? It's massive, it can't just have disappeared."

It's always such a shock when vacation is over. It's as if in the last seven weeks off school, we've forgotten how to do the simplest things: get up, eat breakfast, put on our clothes, and get out of the house. Instead, we're falling over each other in the tiny kitchen.

Dad's already gone. He works in a small architects' firm in Lowell, planning people's apartment conversions and extensions. People get out of Littlehaven as fast as they can in the mornings. He's usually off early to beat the traffic.

The doorbell. It's Grace. I shovel Corn Flakes into my mouth. I'm ready to go.

I used to hate school, well, not hate it, but not feel like I belonged there. I could do the work, I never failed anything, was never called in for a "little talk" with one of the teachers. But I was . . . lost, empty. Like a black-and-white outline of a person. Grace changed all that. Grace colored me in.

This morning Grace whirls into our kitchen at top

speed and almost collides with Mom. But Mom doesn't mind, she just laughs. People never seem to get upset with Grace. There's something about being around her that means you can't stay serious for too long.

So all Mom says is, "Whoa, slow down. You must be excited about the first day back."

"Sorry, Mrs. P!" says Grace, using one of the nicknames only she uses for my parents—Mr. and Mrs. P, instead of Mr. and Mrs. Palmer. I try and avoid calling Grace's mom anything. I'm not sure I even know her first name and coming up with a nickname wouldn't feel right. In my head, she's always just "Grace's mom."

"Hey, Jamie." Grace stops, looks over his shoulder, and points at the back of the cereal box. "Look in that corner, you'll find 'crocodile.' And now, Izzy . . ." She grabs me, twirls me round, and gives me two huge theatrical air kisses—*mwah, mwah*—and strikes a pose. "Let's go and meet our fate. Wish us luck."

"Bye, Izzy," says Mom, stopping to smooth down my blazer and kiss me on the cheek. She looks very serious for a second, her eyes tired and sad, but she quickly snaps back to normal. "Have a good day, my grown-up girl. Have a good year."

"Oh, god," says Grace, as the door slams behind us.

"Yesterday was a nightmare. I mean it. My mom made me go to church *all* day. Like, hours and hours. It was a special welcome service for the new pastor, and I thought it was never, ever going to end. And then there was a lunch that was okay, I suppose, but I couldn't even message you because my phone was out of battery."

I think Grace's church is great, even though I've only been once. In the spring, Mom and Dad went away to a hotel for their wedding anniversary and I went to stay at Grace's for the night. In the morning, we went to church with her mom. It wasn't what I thought church was like. It was in this warehouse on the edge of Lowell. It looked so plain from the outside, but inside was full of color and music.

The man at the front went on and on, but I didn't really listen to what he was saying—I was too busy looking round. It was like going to the theater or watching a musical, but with all of us in the chorus. There were women in their stiff, colored dresses, the band playing, the choir singing, and everybody dancing and swaying, some even shaking and crying. But I think Grace was a bit embarrassed by it, and she never asked me again.

I haven't got much news for her in return. It's not like we haven't been in and out of each other's houses all summer, and messaging most of the rest of the time. But with Grace, you never have to worry about not having enough to say. She simply goes on talking.

When we're almost at the gates, she stops and clutches my arm. "This year's going to be a good one for both of us, isn't it? I feel it, I feel it in my bones." She high-fives me, and I high-five her back, and we run laughing up to the gates, where everyone is jostling and shouting and ready for the year to begin. "And what's more," she whispers right into my ear as we go in, "this year is going to be the year that Sam Kenner notices me."

I don't doubt it. Not at all. Grace knows how to get noticed.

It's good being back and being in seventh grade. The sixth-graders in their too-big blazers and too-long skirts look bewildered. But we know what we're doing.

That was us last September, Grace and me. A whole year ago. Sitting in alphabetical order in that first assembly: Grace Okafor, Isabel Palmer. And after that we were barely apart.

All of a sudden, I stumble forward, almost tripping over. Grace grabs my arm just in time before I hit the ground. Someone has shoved right into me as they run past, knocking me off balance. I look up to see Lucas Pearce and a couple of his friends a little way ahead, laughing and messing around.

"Hey, Lucas," shouts Grace after him. "Watch where you're going!"

"Watch where you're going!" mimics Lucas in a squeaky voice that sounds nothing like Grace's, but still makes Amir and Charlie laugh like they've heard a really funny joke. "Not my fault Izzy's got such big feet that I nearly tripped over them."

I look down. "Don't worry," I whisper to Grace. "It doesn't matter."

Lucas laughs. "You got nothing to say for yourself, Izzy, or do you just let Little Miss Big Mouth do all the talking for both of you?" The boys run off, pushing and grabbing each other's bags.

"That's one person I haven't missed over the break," mutters Grace. "I hope he keeps out of our way for the rest of this semester."

"Hello, Grace. Hello, Isabel. Good summer vacation? Pleased to be back?" says a cheerful voice behind us. It's Mr. Thomas, my favorite teacher. He runs Drama Club and I'm hoping we've got him for English again this year, too.

"Yes, thanks, Mr. Thomas," we chorus.

Grace takes a deep breath, ready to describe her holidays in full and glorious detail, but Mr. Thomas cuts in first. "I suggest you two have a look at the Drama Club board when you get in," he says. "You might find something there to interest you." He smiles. "Unless you've got lazy over the summer . . . because this could mean hard work."

Chapter Three

"Guys and Dolls?"* says Grace with a shrug. "Well, *I've* never heard of it."

Unlike me, Grace hasn't grown up with Dad's obsession with old musicals: *Guys and Dolls, Singing in the Rain, West Side Story.* Films so old they were made when Nana was a little girl. Films full of drama and music, like a doorway into another world.

Mr. Thomas was right. There *was* something to interest us on the notice board:

Presenting...
St. Mary's one and only Sixth & Seventh Grade Christmas
Production
GUYS AND DOLLS

Singing, dancing, acting, crewing, designing
Auditions: Tuesday, September 10th, 3:30 pm.
in the drama studio.
No experience needed. All welcome.

Joining Drama Club was the first thing Grace and I did together. She told me it would be fun, a laugh. I wasn't sure that I believed her, but I went along anyway. The problem was, I didn't like standing up in front of people. I didn't like getting noticed or being put on the spot. Even when I knew the answer in class, I wouldn't put up my hand because I didn't want everyone to look at me. I could see Grace would make an amazing actor with her loud, careless laugh and her desire to be the center of attention. I'd be much happier hiding at the back, handing out the programs or doing the lights. Drama Club didn't sound like a laugh, it sounded like a panic attack waiting to happen.

But, week by week, in Mr. Thomas's drama studio, with the black drapes and big mirrors and West End posters on the wall, I found that I stopped worrying about people looking at me. Because they weren't looking at shy, boring old Isabel Palmer. I didn't have to be that person anymore. I could be whoever I wanted. I still didn't put my hand up in class, but I could step on a stage and be somebody else—

then it didn't matter who was watching.

Last year, Grace dragged me along to try out for the end-of-year production—and somehow we both got parts in the chorus. Just a handful of lines between us, but that didn't matter. Just being up onstage was the best feeling ever.

Once the last performance was over, we all cried and hugged and wondered how we'd live without each other over the summer. Then Mr. Thomas made us sit in a circle and gave us each two pieces of paper. On one we had to write our best memory of Drama Club to read out to the group: the time when Mr. Thomas was pretending to be overwhelmed by our performance and fell backward off his chair; the time when we all went to Lowell to see *To Kill a Mockingbird*; the time when we tried out different accents, but no one could work out what most of them were supposed to be.

At the top of the other piece of paper, we each wrote our name. We passed these around the circle and we each had to write a message for the person whose name was on the bit of paper, fold it over so no one else could see, and pass it on.

I shoved my paper in my bag and waited till I got home before unfolding it. I lay on my bed and read each comment slowly and carefully. I read where Mr. Thomas had written, *There are great things ahead for you. Believe in yourself.* I read where Grace had written, *SUPERSTAR. BEST FRIENDS FOREVER*, and drawn a pink heart decorated with tiny stars. And I tucked that piece of paper under the corner of my mattress. I didn't need to read it again: I knew it was there whenever I needed it.

As we walk down the road, after our first day in seventh grade, I scroll through the results for *Guys and Dolls* on my phone. "Okay, here we go . . . American musical . . . first staged in 1950 . . ."

"What? That's like a hundred years ago," interrupts Grace.

"Ssh, listen, the film won awards. . . . I'm pretty sure we've got it on an old DVD at home. Do you want to come back and watch it now, and we can pick the best parts to go for? Your mom can't say no, it's the first day, there's no homework yet."

"Yes, that would be brilliant. Would your mom mind?"

"Course not, she says you practically live in our house anyway. Come on."

I unlock the front door and shout out a hello. Then

Grace and I race into the living room, sweep all the DVDs off the shelf by the TV, and quickly sort through them. *Guys and Dolls* isn't there.

"Maybe your mom or dad know where it is, let's go and ask them," suggests Grace.

We go through to the kitchen. There's just Megan, on her phone. No sign of anyone else.

"Where's Dad?" I ask her.

"Doctor's," she says without looking up.

"Again? Where's Mom?"

"Office," and she's back to her phone.

Megan must have had a good first day in sixth grade to be actually talking to me. Or maybe it's because Grace's here and everyone likes Grace. I decide not to push my luck by asking anymore, though.

The office is a grand name for the tiny box room where Mom designs websites on her computer, keeps her files, and does her accounts. Every surface overflows with paper—sketches, invoices, leaflets; it even makes my room look super-neat by comparison. Mom's typing, with the phone crooked on her shoulder. She's a freelance web designer. It sounds like it would be a pretty cool job, but she says it's mostly fussy coding and difficult phone calls with clients where she explains why their site won't work the way they want it to.

17

"Hi, girls. Good first day?" She flicks the phone onto speaker mode and motions for us to come in. As the on-hold music plays, Grace and I do a silly little dance and Mom laughs. "Hmm, I see it *was* a good day. Are you staying for dinner, Grace? I'm afraid it's only pizza."

"Yes, please, Mrs. P."

"Actually, Mom, we're looking for *Guys and Dolls* on DVD, do you know where it is? It's the school production and auditions are next week. We want to get ready right now," I say all in a rush. "There's not much time to practice."

"We haven't watched that for years." She looks thoughtful. "If it's not on the living room shelf, then it's in a bag on top of my wardrobe, with all the stuff that's on its way to the charity shop. You can go and look, but don't make too much of a mess, okay? And, Grace, don't forget to text your mom and see if it's all right for you to stay, I know she'll be expecting you back."

At that moment, the music stops and a tinny little voice comes out of the speaker, saying, "Hello, Mrs. Palmer, sorry to have kept you waiting. . . ." Mom grabs the phone, and we make our exit to continue our DVD hunt in Mom and Dad's room.

"I love it how your mom just lets you get on with things, your dad, too. They're so laid-back. Not like my mom."

Grace sighs dramatically, sitting on the bed to tap out a message home.

"That's not true," I say. "Mom's always nagging me about homework."

"Yeah, but *all* parents do that. I mean, with my mom, she always has to be so *involved* in everything. Wanting to know exactly what I'm doing, giving me advice all the time, asking questions about every little thing that happens at school."

This makes me laugh, because that description sounds as much like Grace herself as it is like her mom.

I'd never say it out loud, but sometimes I wish my mom was more like Grace's. It's not that Mom doesn't care about what we're up to, Megan, Jamie, and me. It's just she's not someone who says much. Maybe she simply expects us to know about what she's thinking or feeling, without her needing to say it. Or maybe it's different with Grace and her mom because it's only the two of them, no little brothers or big sisters to get in the way.

"It's not funny." Grace pouts. "I hope it'll be okay to have dinner here. Mom's probably made some special fancy meal or something but I'd rather just have pizza in front of the TV with you."

I don't say anything. I love Grace's mom's meals, with

the mountains of fluffy rice and rich sauces, and home-made cake for dessert. And I love the way she seems to enjoy watching you eat almost as much as eating herself, pressing extra helpings on you before you even finish the first mouthful, explaining what spices have gone in and where each recipe has come from. I can't imagine *her* complaining about my enormous appetite.

Grace reaches up on tiptoes to the top of the wardrobe and grabs hold of a carrier bag. DVDs, books, and some old clothes of Jamie's cascade to the floor. I can't believe Mom is planning to clear some of these out. There are films here that I used to watch over and over again: *Mary Poppins*, *Aladdin*, even *Frozen* . . . I suppose they *are* a bit childish now, but Jamie might still like them. Just looking at the covers makes me think of rainy Saturday afternoons, snuggled up with Dad, Mom, and Megan, singing along. That feels like a long time ago, doing stuff together as a family. I manage to sneak out a few favorites, but we still can't find *Guys and Dolls*.

"Are you sure your mom said everything was on the *top* of the wardrobe? Maybe she meant to look at the back of the wardrobe as well?" asks Grace, as she repacks the bag and carefully balances it just where she found it. "We should check."

"Well, I don't know. . . ." I start to say, but Grace's already opened the wardrobe door and is rummaging around at the bottom. She pulls out a canvas bag that has been shoved in the back.

"Look, maybe it'll be in here?" she says hopefully. She unzips it to reveal a couple of dresses, along with a skirt and top, underwear, and a pair of pink high-heeled shoes. We both stare at them, and then Grace shakes out one of the dresses, holding it up against herself and feeling the silky material between her fingers. I have never seen my mom wear any of these. I can only remember one or two occasions I've seen her in a dress at all. Jeans and sneakers, yes, sometimes a suit when she goes to meet a client, but never a dress. Mom's quite small, too. I'm almost as tall as she is. These clothes would be much too big for her.

Finally, Grace breaks the silence. "I'm not being funny, Izzy, but did your mom used to be massive?"

I don't know why, but just looking at these clothes makes me feel weird. Like reading someone's diary or overhearing a private conversation. They feel secret. And I want them back in the bag, out of sight in the wardrobe. I want not to have found them in the first place.

I shrug, and quickly start packing them away. I can see Grace is itching to try on the shoes—also much larger than

Mom's—but just as she reaches for them, her phone beeps. It's her mom saying she can stay to eat. While she's replying, I shove the shoes in the top of the bag, zip it up tightly, and push it back where we found it.

I hear footsteps coming up the stairs, and feel suddenly guilty, like I've done something wrong. There's an uneasy, creeping feeling in my stomach.

Mom sticks her head around the door, brandishing a DVD. "Honestly, you two, you can't see what's in front of your noses," she says. "I had a quick look and it was right there on the shelf with all the others. Still, at least you've kept things neat in here. Come on, no need to look so startled, pizza's ready. Let's eat."

I slam the door behind us and quickly run down the stairs.

Chapter Four

It's a week since the auditions, and time has been moving extra slowly. But today Mr. Thomas is posting the results. Finally. I'm itching to find out what parts we got, if we even got parts at all.

But first it's French and history, then double chemistry, which feels like it will never, ever end. At last, the final bell goes and the weekend's started. I dash through the corridors, dodging sixth-graders with their lost looks and enormous bags, to the drama studio. Grace gets there at exactly the same time as me, and we skid to a stop, panting, in front of the notice board. The results are here.

Grace and I have watched *Guys and Dolls* seven times now. We know which are the best parts, the ones we want.

I don't believe it at first. I have to check twice to make

sure it's really true. But it is—it's just like we hoped. I'm Sarah Brown, the serious Salvation Army officer who loosens up and finds love as the show goes on. Grace is Miss Adelaide, just as big a part, but more sassy, more Grace's style than mine.

A tiny part of me wonders if I can really do this. It's so different from last year—there'll be lots of lines to learn and scenes to rehearse. What if I'm not good enough? What if I mess it up for everyone else? But then Grace grabs me, and the worries fade away as we shriek and hug and jump up and down. This year is going to be amazing. We are the stars.

There's a little crowd at the notice board by now, and people are jostling to see where their names are on the list. I can tell Sam Kenner's arrived, because Grace starts to talk more loudly and get all giggly. He doesn't need to push in, as he's tall enough to see right over everyone else's heads. Grace's gone on and on about him since the start of last summer.

"I *said*, excuse me," says a sharp voice behind me. I turn around and see Mia Harrison from our year, her hands on her hips and a scowl on her face.

"Sorry," I say, moving out of her way. "I didn't hear you. Are you looking for your part on the list?"

"Well, what else would I be doing here?" she snaps back, pushing past me.

Mia can be ever so polite, even charming, especially when adults are around. She's the sort of girl that parents say you should try to be more like. But when she thinks no one's looking, she can be really mean. She hangs around with our group, but it always feels like she only wants to be with us until someone more interesting comes along.

She turns to Grace and me. "Oh, I see you two have done well. All that sucking up to Mr. Thomas must have paid off." Then she tosses her hair and strides away.

I was so excited with my part that I'd forgotten to look down the rest of the list. I check where Mia's name is—she's General Cartwright, the sour, bossy Salvation Army officer. It's a good part and it totally suits her, but no wonder it made her cross. She'll have wanted one of the more glam roles—like mine and Grace's.

The big shock is Nathan Detroit, Miss Adelaide's loser boyfriend—it's Lucas Pearce, the least likely person ever to be in a leading role. So much for wanting to keep out of his way this year. Sam Kenner is Sky Masterson, the one Sarah Brown falls in love with. Then there's a whole list of gangsters and dancers.

"Look, Sam," says Grace. "You've got a great part."

"Yes." He looks down at Grace and smiles his slightly crooked smile. "You've done well, too."

Sam never says much, but he doesn't need to. He's one of those people who looks at home in any situation, while seeming slightly detached from what's going on around him. I think that's why he's so good at drama: He just does what he wants to do and doesn't care if people think he looks stupid. And because *he* doesn't worry that he looks stupid, no one else thinks he does either. He doesn't spend all his time joking around, like most of the boys in our class. It's one of the reasons why Grace is so into him. Not just his blue eyes and the fact he's taller than any of the other boys. I think it's that he's a bit like her, not afraid to say what he thinks or do what he believes is right. Not like me, always worried what people are going to think if I even say a word.

On the way home, Grace is full of what Sam said, what he meant, what she's going to say to him at the first rehearsal, what the costumes might be like and why on earth Mr. Thomas chose Lucas Pearce for one of the main parts.

I can't wait to get home. I know Mom and Dad will be delighted. They both love musicals, for starters. But more than that, they were both so relieved when I joined

Drama Club. They tried not to show it, but I know they were worried about me starting St. Mary's. Even though they never said it, I could tell. They were worried how their quiet little Izzy would fit in at such a huge and hectic place. So different from Megan, who just took it all in her stride. And here I was, not just fitting in, but going to be star of the show.

"This is the best day of my life," I announce, as soon as I get through the door. Mom and Dad are both in the living room, and Jamie's sitting on the sofa watching cartoons. "Guess what happened, guess!" I demand.

"Oh, I don't know, go on, Izzy, sit down and tell us all about it," says Dad quietly. He sounds odd. I look at him closely, and there are bags under his eyes like he hasn't slept all night. Maybe he's home so early because he's not feeling well.

Even so, I'm a bit disappointed that he won't play along and guess like he used to when I was little and I came home with news from school. He always used to come up with silly guesses that made me laugh like, "You're going on a space mission to Mars," or, "All school dinners have been replaced by fries and chocolate pudding," until I gave in and told him what had really happened. Perhaps he thinks I'm too grown-up for games now. Or perhaps, I wonder, is it him that's changed, not me? Lately, he's seemed so much more serious about everything.

"Oh, all right then, I'll tell you," I say, but I'm still too excited to sit down. "They put up the audition results and . . . Grace and I have got the best parts. I'm Sarah Brown, and she's Miss Adelaide. We'll have loads of lines to learn, and some songs. Rehearsals start next week, and there are three shows right before the end of the school year. It's going to be so, so brilliant."

"Can I come to your show?" says Jamie, looking up from the screen.

"Of course, Jamie, you can sit in the front row, if you like," I reply. Mom and Dad still sit there in silence. A second too late, Dad stands up.

"That's wonderful, Izzy, I'm so proud," he says, giving me a big hug. "Isn't that great news, Kath? I think you'll be a star." But when I look up at his face, he doesn't seem like someone who's heard great news. His smile is stretched on. I can feel all the joy I had evaporating away.

Dad coughs awkwardly. "Well, actually, I've got some news, too." He looks at Mom, then corrects himself. "*We've* got some news. I mean, we've got something we need to talk about as a family. Today. Once Megan's home. It's nothing to worry about, really."

28

And, of course, saying there is nothing to worry about instantly makes me worried. I run through all the nightmare scenarios in my head: we're moving, Dad's lost his job, they're splitting up, he's got an incurable disease—that must be why he looks so pale. If I've thought about the worst that can happen then I can be ready for whatever's coming. Just as I'm starting to worry that all these things could have happened at once and we're going to be left homeless orphans, the door slams.

Before Megan has the chance to dash upstairs to her room, Mom calls her back. I hear them murmuring in the hallway, as Dad asks me questions about the show, about things I've already told him, like when the rehearsals are, and about things I haven't yet, like who else is in it.

Parents aren't supposed to have favorites, everyone knows that. But everyone knows that's not true either. Mom and Megan have always been close. Even at the moment, when Megan refuses to speak to almost everyone, including me, she will still listen grudgingly to Mom. I don't know what it is that makes Megan so angry about everything. When I asked Dad, he just said that's how things are sometimes when you're sixteen, and soon she'll get tired of it and start being a normal human being again. I hope she gets tired of it soon. Maybe starting her junior year will make a difference.

I'm Dad's favorite. Or maybe he's mine. Generally it's him, not Mom, I want to talk to, or sit and watch TV with, when school's been tough or Megan's been annoying me. Mom wants me to be all grown-up and responsible, and I like that sometimes, but with Dad I can relax and just be me.

And Jamie? I think we all forget about Jamie sometimes. That sounds awful. It's not like we literally forget him, no one's ever left him behind in the supermarket or anything, but he's so much younger. Megan and I have always been there to look after him, not to play with him. He's what Mom calls an "after-thought."

"Cup of tea?" says Dad, and he goes out of the room to fart around making tea for him and Mom and Megan. Jamie tries it on by asking for a second grape soda, and—to his surprise—he gets it. I don't want anything.

Once we're all sitting down, it's a bit awkward. We're not really a sitting-down sort of family, someone's usually dashing in or on their way out.

Megan picks at a large hole in her black tights. Jamie spins the wheels of a toy car against the arm of the chair.

"I know this feels a bit strange," says Dad, his voice shaking a little. "But there's something we need to talk about, as a family. It affects me the most, and your mom, but it will affect you, too. I want you to be able to ask us any questions you need to, okay?" We nod, no less confused, but all listening now.

"Well," says Dad slowly. "Have you heard the word 'transgender' before?"

"Yeah—so what?" says Megan, looking up. My brain is whirring. This isn't what I expected. I don't have a clue what Dad is talking about or why.

"Being transgender or being trans," says Dad, "is a way of describing how someone might feel that they are born in a body that doesn't match their true gender. So, you might look like a man but you know you're a woman inside or people think you're a woman but really you know you are a man."

"Fascinating," says Megan sarcastically. "But what's this all got to do with us?"

Dad sighs. "*I'm* transgender," he says, trying and failing to keep his voice from wobbling even more. "What that means is, well, it means what I've known for a long time. That my body and who I am inside don't match up. So I've been living as a man, in a man's body, but actually, I'm a woman." He turns to me as well and looks at us all seriously. "I'm going to start hormone treatment in a few months, and eventually surgery, so gradually my body will change to match who I am. But first I need to start living as a woman. Now."

He glances at Mom, and she nods encouragingly. Jamie's staring into space, I don't think he's really getting it. Megan's sitting dead still now, but I can feel waves of tension coming off her. And me? I feel like all the breath has been knocked right out of me.

One image fills my mind and I can't think of anything else: the bag, the shoes, the too-big clothes. They weren't Mom's after all—they were Dad's. It all makes sense. Except, right now, nothing makes any sense at all.

"It's nothing to be ashamed of, it's nothing dirty, it doesn't make me ill," continues Dad quickly. "But I know it's hard to get your head around this, and that's why it's taken me so long to tell you. It's not going to change anything about how much I love you. But, well, I'm sorry."

He stops. It's like he's come to the end of the speech he's been practicing. He's recited his lines, and now it's our cue. Except there's no script. There's no playwright to tell you what's happening next, or drama teacher to tell you how to deliver your next line. There's no band ready to play the next song. Just silence.

"Is it like Spider-Man?" says Jamie. "Like, there's Peter

Parker and there's Spider-Man. And Peter Parker's really Spider-Man, but no one knows that he is. Like you're a woman, but you look like a man and no one knows about you either?"

"What the . . ." mutters Megan, attacking her tights even more aggressively. "You're *not* a woman, are you? You're our dad. A man." Her voice rises. "How are you going to turn yourself into a woman? How can you 'know' that's what you are when you're not? Is this just some sick joke?"

Megan storms out of the living room, not waiting for any answers, and stomps up the stairs. She slams the door of her bedroom extra-hard. Mom and Dad exchange glances, before Mom gets up to follow her.

Dad turns to me. "Izzy?"

My heart is racing and my head is full of questions, but I don't know how to start asking any of them, so instead of saying anything, I just shrug and try to smile. Dad puts his arm round me, and says, "You're a good girl, Izzy, I promise this is all going to be okay," and we sit there awkwardly for a bit.

Finally, he gets up. "I know it's a lot to take in. But if you think of something later, you can always talk to us. How about I make us all a sandwich? Grilled cheese, Jamie?"

Jamie nods eagerly. He gets irrationally excited about grilled cheese. He'd have it on his Corn Flakes if he could.

"Izzy, what about you?"

"Maybe later," I say. "Is it okay if I just go to my room now?"

I can't eat anything. It seems like hours since I got home from school, full of excitement about being in the show. It seems like days. But it's only half past five. I carry three untouched cups of tea back into the kitchen.

Back in my bedroom, I slump on the floor, leaning against the side of the bed. I suddenly feel tired, too tired even to move.

This must have been going on in Dad's head for months, even years, and I didn't know. I feel so stupid. I don't want him to change. But maybe it's too late, maybe he's always been a different person and I didn't even notice and now there's nothing I can do. My fists are clenched and I can feel my nails digging into my palms. More than anything, I wish he hadn't told us. I wish everything was just like it was before.

I reach for the piece of paper tucked under the mattress, the one with the messages from Drama Club. Normally, reading it makes me feel better. But all I can think about now is what they'd say if they knew my dad . . . what? If they knew he was having a sex change, is that what this is? Would they still like me then? Or would they giggle and whisper and say stuff behind my back? Is Megan right? Is this a sick joke?

Then I spot the new message icon flashing on my phone from earlier. It's from Grace. Of course.

What did yr mom & dad say about the show??
How u feeling bout playing s's girlf? don't forget he's mine. Ha ha

I stare at the message for a while, and then turn my phone off without messaging her back. I can't imagine telling anyone, even Grace, about this right now. What would I say?

Eventually, I drag myself downstairs. Mom, Dad, Jamie, and I eat supper on our knees in front of the TV, picking at our food. The laughter from the studio audience sounds even louder and faker than usual. No one says where Megan is. Mom asks me a bit more about *Guys and Dolls* and I answer her, but it's like I'm just saying the lines. I don't know if anyone's really listening.

I can't help stealing glances over at Dad. Imagining him with different clothes, different hair. Some woman sitting there instead of my dad. But when he looks back at me, I just look down at my plate again.

The sky outside's really dark and it's starting to rain. I can see from my window the houses on the other side of the road turning on their lights and drawing their curtains, even though it's still early.

I wonder what people would think if they could see inside our house right now. If they could take the front off, like a doll's house, and see our little figures moving around inside. Dad loading the dishwasher in the kitchen, Jamie playing in the living room, Mom in her office and Megan and me in our bedrooms. Just like a normal family. All in the same house, but everyone separate. No one talking. But everyone thinking about the same thing. Will we ever be a normal family again?

Chapter Five

I t's Saturday morning. I wake up to the sound of rain drumming on the roof and shouting downstairs. I can't make out the words, but I can hear the up and down of Megan's raised voice, and the softer murmur of Mom's in response. Something's nagging at me ... something I forgot to do or something someone said ... and then I remember. Of course. Dad. I wish I could hide under the duvet all day and pretend that none of this is happening.

By the time I come downstairs in my robe, it's Dad who's speaking. Megan's standing by the door, arms folded, looking ready to storm out again.

"I know this is really hard, Megan, and I wouldn't be transitioning if I felt I had any choice. Please believe that." His voice is pleading now. "I've spent too long pretending that it doesn't matter. I've been to see the doctor and she agrees, and I've been having counseling. Mom and I have talked it all through. I wanted you to know as soon as I was sure this was the right thing."

"I see," says Megan. "So we're the last to know."

I glance up at Mom's face. She's pale and she's biting her lip.

Jamie says, "Are you going to start wearing dresses now? Like dressing up?"

"Yes, sometimes. And sometimes I'll wear jeans and T-shirts—like Mom," says Dad. "But, yes, I will start wearing women's clothes. Although it won't be dressing up, it'll just be my normal clothes. There is one more thing. It won't really make sense for people to call me 'he' or 'him' anymore, will it? So I'll be asking everyone to start using 'she' and 'her.'"

Megan looks horrified.

"It's okay if you forget sometimes," continues Dad. "I know this is all a lot to get used to."

"Izzy, are you okay?" says Mom, looking over at me.

When I speak, my voice comes out all small and squeaky, like when I'm worried about answering a question in class. This is the question I've been wondering and worrying about all night. This is the worst possible thing. I don't want to ask it because I don't want to hear the answer: "Will you two split up?"

"No," says Mom, a bit too loudly. "No. Dad and I made a promise eighteen years ago, and we're not going to break that promise now, whatever happens. Okay? No one's splitting up."

"So, who else knows?" I ask.

"Just us at the moment. And the doctor, and the counselor I've been seeing, like I said. But I'm going to talk to Mark tomorrow, because I'll need to start going to work as a woman, too." Mark is Dad's boss, a large, jolly man with a big beard. "And we'll need to talk to your teachers...."

"No," interrupts Megan. "Absolutely not. You are not going anywhere near school with this. I can't believe you even thought it. This is such a nightmare for me, why couldn't you have waited two years till I've got out of this stupid place? Why are you trying to ruin everything?"

"Megan," says Mom sharply. "I know you're upset, but we're trying to do the right thing by you all. We're not trying to ruin your life. We need to talk to your school, just in case anything happens, or anyone says anything, they can look out for you. That's all."

"I don't *need* anyone to look out for me," shouts Megan.

"I'm not a baby. Maybe Jamie and Izzy do, but I don't. All *I* need is to be left alone."

Once Megan's gone back to her room, I don't really want to stick around either, but there's one other question I need to ask: "Can I tell Grace?"

My phone beeps angrily when I switch it on. There's a string of messages from Grace, ending with: earth calling Izzy—where are you?

I message back: sorry, really weird at home, Dad's done something strange

The phone beeps: parents R strange, what's he done??

Dad's said it's okay to tell Grace, though not anyone else yet. But now that I can, I don't know what to say.

he says

i think

it's hard 2 xplain

After a few minutes of staring at the screen, writing something, then hammering "Delete" and starting again, I give up and message: can u meet me at the swings in 10 mins?

I figure no one's in the mood to nag me to do my homework, so I'm free. Labelling the main features of a gurdwara or reading another chapter of *Of Mice and Men* can wait.

The park's midway between my house and Grace's. It's still pouring with rain. I can feel a few drops sliding down the back of my neck and it makes me shiver.

I get there first. There's no one around, apart from a few dads pushing strollers with waterproof covers on. It's still too early and too wet for most people to be out.

I rub the water off with my sleeve, then hop onto a swing and push off hard, soaring high and dipping back. I feel free. Like if I swing fast enough or stretch high enough, I can leave behind Dad and Mom, and everything that's happened. I can fly.

I shut my eyes and just concentrate on the feeling of the wind in my hair and listening to the sound of the chains creaking. When I open them, Grace is there, swinging beside me.

"So, what's up?" she says and smiles. She adjusts her speed so that we are swinging alongside each other. "It's soaking out here."

I still don't know how to start, but when I begin talking, it all comes out in a rush. "So, I got home yesterday, and there's Dad and Mom and Jamie and Megan, and Dad wanted us to sit down and talk," I say. "He looked awful. And then he started saying all this stuff about not being a man, but being a woman in a man's body, and how he's going to start wearing dresses, or at least sometimes, and how he's going to have a sex change. At least he didn't say about the sex change, but he did say something about hormones and doctors, so that must be what he means. . . . And then this morning, no one's talking, just shouting. . . ."

It's easier to keep swinging as I talk. Then I don't have to look at Grace's face and try and guess what she's thinking. And it's easier to keep talking than to stop and listen to what she's going to say.

"Oh my god," says Grace finally. "Oh my god." When I look up, I can see her eyes are wide. "What's your mom going to do?"

"They're not splitting up, that's what she says. But I don't know. Jamie's fine, he thinks it's all about dressing up, and Megan's in a total state about it."

"Oh my god," says Grace again. "Sorry. But, oh, Izzy, what about you?"

I start to say, all calm and collected, "I don't know how I feel yet. . . ." and then all of a sudden, something breaks and I'm crying and crying and I don't know how to stop. I'm crying so much that I have to stop swinging because I don't have any breath left and my arms and legs feel all wobbly.

I hear myself sobbing and gasping and snuffling. I know

that somehow this crying is connected to the crying I overheard on the first night of the holidays—and tried to forget about all summer.

Grace doesn't say "oh my god" again, she doesn't try and joke me out of it or ask me more questions. She doesn't say anything. She gets off her swing, and crouches awkwardly on the wet ground in front of me and holds me, until the crying stops.

Chapter Six

I wake up glad it's Monday; this weekend has been grim. It rained so much that all I could do was bum around the house. Grace's constant stream of messages and pictures helped to take my mind off things, but sometimes I'd spot something—like a photo of me and Dad or a pair of his ordinary running shoes sitting in the hallway—and suddenly, for no reason, I'd burst into tears.

Downstairs, it's a normal Monday morning. The same arguments over who's used up the last of the milk or left their shoes in the middle of the floor. The same scramble for the bathroom and search for a clean shirt. Dad's gone to work early. Jamie's happily singing away to himself. Mom's still looking white as a sheet, but she's putting on a brave face. I probably look pretty awful, too, after all the crying I've done this weekend. Megan looks like thunder, but nothing new there.

Despite the messages, I'm half worried that Grace won't turn up after what I told her on Saturday morning. What if she's been thinking about it, and decided that she doesn't want to be my friend anymore? I couldn't bear that. It would be worse than anything Dad could've said. Perhaps I shouldn't have told her. She'd still find out, though, wouldn't she? Sooner or later she'd know.

But the doorbell rings as usual. And there's Grace, same as ever, full of bounce and bubble. I'm almost bursting with the relief that she's my friend, *still* my friend, and that I didn't make a terrible mistake in telling her.

Once the door's shut behind us, she grabs my arm and pulls me close, whispering rapidly. "Izzy, I've been doing some research, about what you told me. I've been googling. Turns out there are *loads* of people like your dad. Did you know that? Oh, and you don't say 'sex change,' that's not right. It's 'transitioning' instead."

Why didn't I think of finding all this out? I wonder. Typical Grace, it's *my* family crisis, but *she's* the one taking charge.

I'm glad she is, though. I don't have the energy to get through this by myself.

"But there aren't loads of people *here*, are there? Not in Littlehaven. Tell me one person you've ever heard of who's transgender in Littlehaven," I challenge her. I can't help it, even though she's done all this to be nice and kind and thoughtful, I can't see what difference it will make. "Maybe in London or in New York or somewhere, there're loads, but not here," I continue.

"Yeah, but you might not even know," insists Grace. "Some of the pictures, you'd never know that they'd not always been a woman. There's that journalist. And there's a TV chef. And there's Caitlyn Jenner—she's old but she looks amazing. Those dresses we found, well, I've been thinking, they must have been his, mustn't they? They were nice clothes. Your dad will look fine, honestly."

"I suppose," I say, unconvinced.

"And look, Izzy, he's not going anywhere, is he? That's what he's said, and your mom, too. He still loves you. It's only this one thing that's going to change. That's all."

I nod, concentrating hard on not crying. "It's one big thing, though. . . ."

"Yeah, but at least you've got a dad," says Grace quietly.

I stop walking, surprised. Grace hardly ever talks about her dad, not even to me. All I know is that he left when she was a baby. There aren't even any photos of him around her house. It's just her and her mom. Always has been. I glance over at her, but it's clear she doesn't want to say anymore now.

I suppose she's right, but that doesn't stop me worrying about people finding out.

"I know," I reply. "But can you even imagine what people in this dump are going to say when the news goes public? Remember what it was like when Mr. Thomas said all that stuff about Shakespeare writing love poems to a man, and all those famous playwrights being gay? Everyone laughed and said how disgusting it was, and Lucas Pearce started reading them out in a funny, lisping voice and flapping his hands around." I stop. I'd laughed, too, even though the poems were beautiful and I didn't really find Lucas funny. "And that was just because Shakespeare liked both men and women. This is much, much worse."

"Not everyone laughed," says Grace. "Sam didn't laugh, do you remember?" The picture comes back into my mind of Sam sitting there, looking more and more angry, before finally telling Lucas to shut up. Sam was all right, though, no one messes around with Sam.

"You won't say anything, will you? Not to anyone." I face her, deadly serious now. St. Mary's uniforms are starting to appear all around us as we walk past the bus stop. "Promise me."

"Cross my heart and hope to die," says Grace. "Let's go. I've got Spanish first, and I've hardly looked at any of the vocab. What have you got first?"

"Math."

"Yuk, even worse! I bet you've done your homework though, haven't you?" She sighs dramatically, without waiting for an answer. "I don't know why we even need to know what half these places are in Spanish anyway—I'm hardly going to want to go to the dentist while I'm on vacation in Spain, am I?"

Grace's pretending to ask me for directions in Spanish when Olivia and Sheetal, a couple of the girls from Drama Club, come running up behind us. I've almost forgotten all about the show so, for a moment, I think they're going to say something about Dad. Then I remember they don't know. Perhaps they wouldn't even care if they did. Some chance.

"You two have got great parts," says Olivia, swinging her long blonde plait over her shoulder. "Have you started learning any of the songs yet?"

"What part have you got?" I ask her.

"I'm just in the chorus," replies Olivia. "But I saw Mr. Thomas in the corridor, and he says we've got some lines, too, even if we haven't got separate parts. There'll still be stuff to learn, but not too much—and we're in loads of songs."

"What do you think about Lucas?" asks Sheetal. "I didn't think he'd get such a big part. I don't think I've even heard him sing before—although he'll be perfect as a gangster!"

"Weird, isn't it?" says Grace, making a face. "I thought Lucas always said that drama sucked. Now I've got loads of scenes with him—*and* I have to pretend to be in love with him. Yuk."

"Yeah, you'll have to be *really* good at acting to do that!" says Sheetal, and everyone laughs.

Grace nudges me. "It's all right for Izzy, playing Sam's girlfriend." I can feel myself blushing. I check Grace's face to see if she really doesn't mind, or if she's secretly mad about the part I've got and the chance to spend all that time with Sam. But her smile looks genuine. I think she just wanted to move the conversation on to Sam. It's not like I even want to go out with him. Why would I want to compete with Grace?

Sheetal is still talking about Lucas. "Not just him— Charlie and Amir are in it, too. I think Mr. Thomas had a word with them, persuaded them that they wouldn't have to prance around in tights or whatever they were so worried about. Maybe he said that taking part would get him off their backs about how poor their English grades are!"

I tense up when she says "prance around in tights" and go quiet, as the others carry on chatting about *Guys and Dolls* until we get inside. Grace heads upstairs to the language labs, I follow Olivia and Sheetal to Mrs. Dalton's math lesson. At first, I think I won't have space in my head for anything else apart from the show and Dad, but somehow I get absorbed in working out equations and plotting graphs. I like math, although I wouldn't admit it to scary Mrs. Dalton.

I like that a right answer is always right. It's not a matter of opinion whether it's right or not, it simply is. And if you don't get the right answer first time, the problem stays the same, so you can just go back and tackle it again. There's always another chance.

As the day passes, worrying about Dad moves from the front of my mind, to settle like a weight at the bottom of my stomach. Even when I'm not thinking about it, it's there in the background. I'm not sure how I feel about seeing him tonight.

We're not a family that talks about every little emotion, or many emotions at all. But this weekend, we've talked and shouted and cried more than ever before. And then we've been more silent than ever before, too. It's the silence that scares me most. What if we've got nothing to say to each other anymore? What if this doesn't just change one thing, like Grace said, but changes everything?

Chapter Seven

Dad's at work when I get back from school, so I don't have to face him yet. I don't know where Megan is, but Mom and Jamie are home, sitting on the living room floor, playing checkers. I can hear by Jamie's whoops of delight that Mom's letting him win.

When Mom hears me come in, she leaps to her feet.

"Well done, Jamie, I think you won that one," she says. "Why don't you tidy up the game while I get a drink for me and Izzy?" She looks at me anxiously. "You'd like a drink, wouldn't you, love?"

I don't really, I just want to go straight up to my room, but instead I nod and follow Mom into the kitchen.

"So how was school?" she asks, reaching into the cupboard for a couple of mugs. She drops a tea bag into one, and spoons hot chocolate powder into the other.

"Ah, you know. . . ." I say, shrugging. "All right, I suppose."

"And how's Grace? Still excited about the play?"

"Yeah, I guess so. First rehearsal's tomorrow after school, so we'll get our scripts and everything then, I think."

We lapse into silence. The only sound is the kettle boiling.

"You said you were going to tell Grace," she says finally. "About Dad's transition . . ." I can tell that she finds the word "transition" really difficult to say. She's got the same look on her face, like when she's taken a bite of something too hot or too cold. "I wondered, did you talk to her? Was that okay? I'm not trying to pry, Izzy, honestly, I just want to make sure you're all right."

"I'm fine," I say. "I'm fine. Grace was fine." I know Mom wants to know more, but I really don't want to talk right now, I just want to be by myself.

"That's great," Mom says, handing me the hot chocolate. "It's really important to have friends who can understand, who you can talk to. It's the same for me and your dad, it's really helped us." She pauses, stirs her tea. "There's a new friend actually, someone we'd like you to meet. She's coming over for lunch on Saturday. Her name's Vicky."

This is interesting. And unusual. It's not often someone new gets invited over. Mom and Dad are always friendly with everyone, but they don't seem to have close friends. Not friends they see all the time, anyway.

Dad goes out to the pub sometimes with Mark and the others from work. Mom's best friend, Chloe, moved to America to get married before I was born. She and Mom Skype at strange times of day because they're in different time zones, but we've only met her a couple of times. I can't imagine having a best friend who I don't see all the time. Whenever I say that to Mom, though, she says, "It's not like you and Grace. It's different when you're an adult, you don't need to see your friends every single day. Chloe's there when I need her. Anyway, Dad's my best friend, too, and I see plenty of him!"

We all know the story about how Mom and Dad met. They grew up on the same street and became friends, then boyfriend and girlfriend. They'd been going out at school, and then split up while they were away at college but got back together again and got married a few months after graduating. Megan says it shows a lack of adventure. I think it's really lovely. Sometimes it seems like they only need each other.

54

I hold back my questions about Vicky for now. "Is it okay if I take my hot chocolate upstairs?" I ask. "I'm a bit tired."

Mom hesitates for a moment, about to say something else, but then Jamie comes running in. "You're taking forever," he says, pulling on Mom's arm. "Come and play with me. Izzy, you have to come and play, too." He grabs my hand. "I've made a hospital, and Mommy's going to be the first patient and then you have to be ill, too. Then I will make you better."

"Well, I'm not sure, Jamie," says Mom, glancing at me. "Izzy's just said she's tired. . . ."

Jamie gives us both a withering look. "Don't be silly. You just have to lie down and be ill. You don't have to *do* anything." He looks so small and so serious that Mom and I both laugh.

"Okay, Jamie," I say, following him into the living room. "I'll come to the hospital, as long as you don't give me any nasty-tasting medicine today."

It's actually the most relaxed I've felt all day, lying on the floor, as Jamie fixes my pretend broken arm, bad knee, and sore throat, but eventually he wanders off, leaving me and Mom to unwind each other's toilet paper bandages.

"Here," says Mom. "Before I forget, I printed off this list of websites. You know, just in case they're helpful." She pulls a piece of paper out of her back pocket and hands it to me. "Just in case there's anything you want to know, but don't want to ask us."

Upstairs, I decide to check out a couple of the sites on Mom's list. I get the feeling she'd find it easier if I found out everything this way, instead of having to ask her. The first one is the best, even though it's just films of people talking about their lives. Most of them seem really normal, they're nice, even funny—a bit like Dad really, despite all being different ages and from different places. I never thought there would be that many other people going through the same thing as us. But on the next site, there are loads of words that I don't really understand, and when I click on the definitions, they just take me to more words that I don't know and need to look up. I stop because it's making me dizzy.

Instead, I decide it's easier to follow Grace's example: do a bit of googling of my own and see what comes up. I find out that she's right about one thing—Caitlyn Jenner does look amazing and super-glamorous. She's still got her career and loads of fans.

But that's not what I want my dad to look like. That's

not what dads are supposed to look like. Especially in Littlehaven. I just want him to look ordinary and normal. To *be* ordinary and normal.

I scroll down the articles to the comments, and they start to blur in front of my eyes until just one or two words stand out. For all the people praising Caitlyn's bravery or saying what a great role model she is, there are loads more that are full of abuse. *Tranny. Heshe. Pervert. Freak.*

I imagine those words whispered in the corridor or scrawled on a bathroom wall. Someone saying them to Jamie or shouting them at Dad. Mom knowing that's what people are thinking inside when they look at our family.

There's a light knock on my door and Dad steps in. I quickly flick my phone off before he sees what I'm looking at.

"Okay if I come in, Izzy?" he asks, and I nod without saying anything.

He sits down on the end of the bed. We're both quiet for a bit.

"I'm sorry I wasn't really switched on about your show on Friday," he says. "I really am so pleased for you, and so proud. I think you're going to be great. Perhaps I could help you with your lines some time? There's a lot to learn for Sarah Brown."

I shrug. I'd love Dad to help with my lines, but I don't say anything.

"And, Izzy, I am so sorry, about springing this on you." I know exactly what he's talking about, without him having to say anything else. "I know it's hard for you," he continues. "That's the last thing I want to happen, for you and I not to be right. I will always love you just the same, I'll always be there for you—and Megan and Jamie—my gender's got nothing to do with that."

"But why now? Why not wait, like Megan said?" I say, twisting and untwisting the edge of my duvet between my fingers.

Dad sighs. "I've been waiting for thirty-nine years," he says quietly. "I've been waiting since before I knew what this was, before I knew it had a name. And I have been having counseling, talking it through with people, for months now. I'm not rushing into this. It was just hard to find the right way to tell you. I know this seems fast to you, but I can't go on waiting. Jamie's five. I can't wait for him to grow up and leave home, even if I could wait for you and Megan. I need to get on with my life, my real life. I can't wait anymore."

"But aren't *we* your real life?" I burst out. "Me, and Megan and Jamie, being our dad, isn't that real life?"

"Yes," says Dad. "Yes, of course it is. But this is, too. It's who I am. And once I can feel comfortable in who I am, I think I can be a better parent to all of you."

"Do you really think this will make you happy?" I ask. "It's just . . ." I hesitate, unsure whether or not to say this. "It's just, I heard you crying, one night, in the summer, I couldn't sleep and I heard and I didn't know. . . ."

"Oh, Izzy," says Dad, reaching out to hold my hand. I let him. "I'd do anything not to upset you." He sighs. "I think I know the night you mean. Mom and I had been talking, going over things again and again. That was the night we finally decided that we had to tell you, but it took the rest of the summer to agree how and when. I guess I was crying because I knew how hard it was going to be, and because I was so tired, Izzy, so tired of keeping secrets. I'm so sorry you heard that. But things will be different—me transitioning is going to make them better, I promise."

It kind of makes sense. "Have you talked to Megan like this?" I ask.

Dad smiles a thin sort of smile and spreads out his hands. "Well, you know Megan. She doesn't really want to talk to me at the moment—or listen to anything I have to say. She's talking to Mom, though. It'll take time, that's okay."

He looks so sad that I want to reach out and hug him. But I'm still angry with him, too. He's supposed to be the grown-up, not me. He's supposed to be the one comforting *me*. The one with the answers. He's supposed to be my dad. And I'm not ready for that to change.

"Look," he says, "I wanted to tell you something else. I spoke to Mark today. He's been really good actually. He says there's no reason why I can't start coming to work as who I really am. He just wants a little bit of time for the others to get used to the idea, see that I'll dress a bit differently and to give me a chance to explain to them about calling me 'she,' that kind of thing. And I'm going to have to change my name, too. I'll be Danielle now...."

I feel so stupid. I can't believe it didn't occur to me straightaway that if Dad's a woman, he'll need a woman's name. I wonder if Megan's thought of that yet and, if not, how she'll react.

I guess going from Daniel Palmer to Danielle Palmer is hardly the biggest change in the world. It's pretty lucky that he has such an easy name to change. Imagine if he was Kevin or Godfrey or Archibald. It's not such a big change, I suppose—but it's yet another thing that means my dad's not really my dad anymore.

"When's that going to happen?" I ask quietly.

"Probably in a couple of weeks." I can hear the edge of nervous excitement in his voice.

A couple of weeks? It's much, much sooner than I'd thought.

"Well, anyway, I'll let you get on with your homework . . . or messaging Grace, or whatever you're up to," he says, standing up.

"Dad?" I ask, just as he opens the bedroom door to go downstairs.

"Yes, Izzy?" He turns back. "What is it?"

"Well, is it okay to still call you 'Dad'? It's just that it feels a bit weird now, you know . . . can you be a woman and be a dad?"

He looks at me. "What do you want to do?"

"I want . . ." My voice has come out all squeaky, so I stop, clear my throat and start again. "I want you to still be my dad."

"Oh, Izzy, I will be always be your dad, okay? Always. Whatever name you call me. You can still call me 'Dad' if you like, or maybe we'll come up with something better." He looks thoughtful. "Oh, except maybe not 'Dad' when we're out and about." He shakes his head. "There's so much to think about, isn't there? But we'll work it out, I promise. We'll work it out together. Now, I need to get the pasta on if we're not all going to die of hunger tonight. I bet you're ravenous already."

And he's out of the door before I have time to get up and give him that hug. So I put my music on loud and lie on my bed, without bothering to turn on the light, and I wait for the meal that he knows is my favorite—macaroni cheese, made Dad's special way, tangy and gooey, with Worcestershire sauce in the mix. He's trying to say he loves me and nothing's really going to change. But it will take more than a plate of pasta to make me believe it.

Chapter Eight

It's the first rehearsal. This is for everyone—from the biggest parts to the smallest—so the drama studio's packed. Even Grace has to shout to be heard above all the noise. Her eyes are darting round, looking for Sam. When she spots him, she grabs me by the hand, and we thread our way through the small groups standing chatting, so that we can be "accidentally" standing right beside him.

There's no chance for Grace to start talking to him, though, as Mr. Thomas stands on a chair, claps his hands, and starts to speak.

"Settle down, settle down." And gradually the noise dies down to a low murmur. "Welcome, cast and crew of *Guys and Dolls*, to the first rehearsal of this year's production." There are a few whoops and cheers.

"For those of you who haven't been in a St. Mary's production before," continues Mr. Thomas, "we're going to have really, really good fun together over the rest of the term, but we're going to work really, really hard as well. We want to give everybody who comes to see us the best possible show. We want them leaving the performance humming the tunes, and happier than when they came in.

"I know that you can all put on a first-class show. And I believe that you will. Whether you're doing the lights, or in the chorus, whether you've got one line or hundreds, every one of you is an important part of this show. Without you playing your part, we can't succeed. We all need to work together." He's got everyone's full attention now.

"We won't be doing much rehearsing today. We'll do a few activities to warm up and get to know each other better, and then I've got scripts and a schedule for each of you to take and a letter home to your parents." He waves a bundle of papers in the air and raises his voice. "*Please* don't lose these. Guard them with your lives. That includes you, Lucas," he says. Lucas's bag is already overflowing with paper; I don't know how he finds anything in there. "Just because your English homework has magic disappearing powers, doesn't mean your script has as well!" Lucas doesn't care, he just laughs.

"Right, are you ready to get moving?" Mr. Thomas asks. "Get into groups according to the month you were born in," he says, and the noise levels start to rise again. "Wait—I haven't finished. Get into groups *without* talking." A groan goes up. "That's your challenge. You can mime or sing or use sign language, you can even dance, if that helps, but you have to communicate without talking. Okay, off you go."

After a lot of shuffling and giggling, we find our way into the right groups. I'm in February with Sheetal, Charlie—and Sam. Grace is on the other side of the room in December, with Mia, Lucas, and a couple of sixth-grade boys. She looks over at me and makes a face. I raise my eyebrows back.

"Now, find a partner in your group," says Mr. Thomas. "And you have two minutes to find out what they did on their last birthday. Starting now . . ."

Instead of turning to Charlie, as I expect, Sam turns straight to me. "So, Izzy, do you want to go first?"

"Er, okay." It feels like answering something in class. I feel my palms getting sweaty, so I wipe my hands quickly on my skirt. "Well, my birthday's actually on Valentine's Day, so it's kind of easy for people to remember. It's a bit embarrassing, too. But my dad says at least that means I'll always get a card on Valentine's Day." I can feel myself blushing.

"So, er, what was the question?" I stutter. "Oh, yes, on my birthday, well, I went ice skating with my whole family. It was really funny. Jamie, he's my little brother, he kept falling over, he's only five, and it made him giggle and giggle. Then it made us all laugh, so he kept doing it, so that we would keep laughing. And then I was laughing so much, I fell over, too! It was freezing, but we went back home and all curled up under duvets on the sofa. Megan, that's my big sister...."

"She's a junior, isn't she?" interrupts Sam.

"Er, yeah, that's right. Well, Megan made me a cake. It's kind of a family tradition, she's done it every year since I was born."

I know I am rattling on and I'm sure Sam can't be interested. It makes me feel warm inside remembering just what a great day my birthday was and how close I'd felt to Mom, Dad, Jamie, and even Megan. Then I remember how different things feel at home now, and I stop talking abruptly.

I notice that Sam's smiling. "Your birthday's on the fourteenth?" he says slowly, raising an eyebrow. "You're older than me! Mine's not till right at the end of the month."

Before he can say anymore, we've run out of time and

Mr. Thomas is back on his chair. He moves us in and out of different groups, but somehow Grace and I never end up in the same one, and I'm not in a group with Sam again either.

We play trust games, act out little scenes, and finish with a game where we have to make faces to express different emotions, like fear, surprise, or anger. I'm paired with Mia for the last game. I don't think either of us needs to act too hard when we have to create faces of disgust or boredom.

Soon it's almost time to go home. "You have been brilliant today, thank you," says Mr. Thomas. "I don't think I'm ever going to forget some of your scary faces." He does a pretend shudder. "Now, before we finish, who knows what happens in *Guys and Dolls*?" About half the hands go up. "Good, so you know what you are getting yourselves in for. And who's seen the film?" Fewer hands this time, but Grace's and mine stay up.

"If you haven't seen it, try to beg, borrow, or buy a copy or just look up the songs on YouTube. I'll be showing a few scenes as part of rehearsals, but it's worth watching the whole thing, if you can. I'm now just going to talk through the story. For those who don't know, it will help you get your bearings. And for those who do, it's a good reminder.

But you all have to stay awake—whenever I mention your character, you need to stand up."

And he tells the story, with Grace, Sam, Lucas, and I bobbing up every few seconds. He also talks about the lights and the costumes, and even the programs, so everyone gets to stand up at some point.

As we get ready to go, Grace hangs back, fiddling with her bag. I think she's just waiting for me, but really she wants to talk to Sam.

"Hi, Sam." He looks down and smiles at her. "Actually, I've got *Guys and Dolls* on DVD. It's really good for learning the lines and everything. You can borrow it some time, if you want. . . ."

"Thanks, Grace, you're the best, that'd be great." He shoulders his bag. "See you both later."

"I'll bring it to next rehearsal!" calls Grace to his back. He turns and nods.

"You don't have a copy of *Guys and Dolls* on DVD," I point out as we walk home.

"Correct!" says Grace. "*I* don't. But *you* do."

"You've promised him *my* DVD?"

"Yeah, come on, we don't need to watch it again, we've seen it so many times. If I get it from your house at the weekend, then I can give it to Sam next week. Perfect."

"Why didn't you go the whole way and invite him round to watch it with you . . . get some popcorn. . . ."

"Don't be stupid. Can you *imagine* what my mom would be like if he came over to my house? Offering him cake every five minutes and asking him what colleges he's looking at and whether or not he goes to church. She'd probably be sitting on the sofa right in between us all evening! I don't want to put him off straightaway."

"You could always ask him over to mine? After all, it's my DVD."

Grace looks like she's considering it.

"Joking!" I say quickly. "Anyway, it's not much fun in my house at the moment. Megan's still not talking to Dad. And Mom and Dad are still discussing the worst idea of the century—do they need to come into school and tell the teachers about Dad or not?"

"You don't *seriously* think they will?" says Grace. "I mean, what's the point? If they are worried about you getting bullied, I'll stick up for you, so will everyone in Drama Club, I know they will. And it's going to be far, far worse having them at school, chatting away to the teachers about all sorts of private stuff. I suppose it wouldn't so bad if it was Mr. Thomas, but imagine talking about it with Mrs. Dalton. . . ." She makes a face.

"I know, I know," I say. "Tell them, not me. They're definitely going into Jamie's school. It's different with grammar school. But we're trying to talk them out of coming into St. Mary's. Well, I'm talking. Megan's mostly shouting and storming around."

We turn down my road and walk in silence for a while, each lost in our own thoughts.

"You know, it's kind of romantic," says Grace, out of nowhere.

"What's romantic?" I ask, puzzled.

"Your parents. I can see for your dad, him being a woman, that's something he, she, really has to do. But what about your mom? It's not her dream, and yet she's sticking by him. I think that's romantic."

"Shut up," I say. "You're talking about my parents. Eurgh."

"Although, it's interesting, isn't it?" she continues thoughtfully. "Like, if your dad's a woman, and he's still with your mom, then does that make your dad a lesbian? Hey, does that make your mom a lesbian, too?"

"Grace, I said shut up. This is seriously freaky. I don't want to talk about this, okay? What if someone hears?"

"Oh, Izzy," says Grace, and she pulls a sad face. It looks so much like one of the faces that Mr. Thomas got us to practice at the end of rehearsal, that it actually makes me laugh. Grace laughs, too.

"Now, never mind parents, we have much more important things to discuss," she says, reassured that I'm not having a total breakdown. "*What* were you and Sam talking about? It's got to have been better than being stuck with moaning Mia, listening to her go on and on about how much better she is than everyone else."

"Oh, nothing much, just stuff about birthdays," I reply.

"You know what this means, though. Now we know Sam's birthday's in February, like yours, he's probably an Aquarius, like you. It's written in the stars. . . ." she says excitedly.

"What is?" I ask, puzzled.

"He's Aquarius and I'm Sagittarius—they're compatible signs!" she exclaims, like this proves her latest crazy theory. "It's one of the reasons we're best friends, and it means that Sam and me are meant to be together."

I wonder about telling her that Sam's birthday is at the end of February, so he's actually a Pisces. But she looks so pleased with herself I decide there's no need.

By this time, we've reached my house. Grace and I usually sit on the front wall chatting for at least another twenty minutes. Dad calls it "chewing the fat," which sounds totally disgusting, and Mom calls it "time wasting." which isn't much better. But today, because of the rehearsal, it's already late, and we both know we need to get moving.

"Only one more day till the weekend," says Grace, with a little cheer. "What are you doing? Do you want to ask your mom and dad about us going shopping on Saturday?"

"Sorry, I can't," I say. "They've got a friend coming over for lunch. It's a bit of a big deal. Mom and Dad are even doing all the cooking. Megan and I have to be there." Grace raises her eyebrows. "I know. We haven't met her before. She's called Vicky. I think they really want to impress her."

"Oh, well, next weekend maybe? I might go with Olivia anyway on Saturday, would you mind? Just to have a look. There's some really cool new stuff I want to try on."

I just shrug in response. To be honest, I usually find shopping with Grace pretty boring. She loves trying everything on, hitting the changing rooms with armfuls of clothes, treating it like a fashion show. She finds things for me as well, and they always look better than what I'd choose for myself. But even so, the best bit is still a milkshake at McDonald's between shops.

Yet I would rather spend the day trailing around the shops with Grace, than at home with Mom and Dad. Especially with this Vicky coming round.

"See you later then," says Grace, and as I get to the door, I hear her calling, "Don't forget the DVD." I turn and give her a thumbs-up and I can see her grinning from halfway down the road.

Chapter Nine

"**W**hy do we have to stick around all day to meet their boring friends?" grumbles Megan to me. I'm trying to ignore her. I'm not feeling too happy about staying in either, but I don't see the point in moaning.

"Dad, how do you know Vicky?" I ask, snacking on another cookie, as he chops piles of carrots.

"We first met a few months ago, at the transgender support group," Dad replies.

Megan's head shoots up from her sketchbook. She's forgotten that she's not talking to Dad. "Hold on a minute. *Re*wind. You met her at the *what*?"

"I've been going to a transgender support group for a little while now," says Dad, slightly sheepishly. "It's over in Norwich," he adds, as if that explains everything.

"When have you been sneaking off there?" accuses Megan.

"Come on, Megan, don't be dramatic, I haven't been sneaking anywhere."

"Well, you haven't exactly mentioned it before, have you?"

Dad takes a deep breath, biting back what he was going to say. "No, maybe I haven't, and I'm sorry. But I'm glad you want to know about it now." Megan snorts. "It's once a month, I head over after work sometimes. It's just a small group, but everyone's very friendly. They've helped me a lot. There's support for partners, too, so Mom's met a few of the people from the group as well."

"Yet more people who knew before us," mutters Megan under her breath, but loud enough for Dad to hear. He pretends not to and carries on talking.

"Anyway, I think you'll like Vicky." He nods at Megan. "You and she have got a lot in common." Megan looks appalled. "Your art, for a start. Vicky manages a gallery in Norwich. Lots of modern pieces, portraits, sculpture, too. You'd like it. And you're both no-nonsense women, you don't let anyone mess you around." Megan tries not to look pleased at Dad's description of her, but I can tell by her shuffling in her seat that she is.

All the time that Dad's been talking, images have been whirling through my mind. What will Vicky look like? What will she act like? Will she be like a Caitlyn Jenner supermodel, or some fat, middle-aged man in women's clothes and dodgy makeup?

"Right," says Dad, interrupting my thoughts. "I'm going up to get changed. Izzy, if I'm not down in fifteen minutes, can you get the veggies going?"

As he heads up the stairs, Megan turns and hisses at me, "What do you think he's going to wear?"

I shrug. Why should it matter what Dad's wearing?

She carries on staring at me.

Suddenly I realize what she means. He's not going to be wearing his normal clothes, is he? If Vicky's from the support group, then she's probably seen Dad in women's clothes before. But *we* haven't.

I go cold inside. Even though I know we're only going to be at home and no one's going to see. It's just clothes, I tell myself as I crumble the rest of my cookies between my fingers.

When Dad comes back downstairs, I don't want to look. As soon as I hear him come in the room, I leap up to the freezer to get out the peas. Before I turn around, I take a deep breath. This is not just an idea anymore. This is really happening and I'm not ready.

But it's not as bad as I thought it would be. He's shaved and put makeup on. He's wearing a blouse and skirt, but nothing too short or too clingy. I hadn't realized how long his hair's been getting, and today it's styled all differently, more feminine somehow.

He looks like Dad, and not like Dad all at once. He doesn't look quite like a woman. He's the wrong shape. But he's not exactly a man either. It's deeply weird.

He looks nervous, like he's worried about how we will react.

Megan says nothing and walks out of the room.

I start to splutter something incoherent about how I like his top, but then Jamie barrels in at top speed, looking for cookies. He stops, looks puzzled at Dad for a few seconds, working out who this stranger in the kitchen is, then shouts out, "Daddy's got boobies!" and jumps up for a cuddle.

"Yes, all right, Jamie, calm down," Dad says, a bit embarrassed. But I think he's pleased that Jamie's just come out and said it. "These are just pretend for now. But when I start taking hormones, that's my medicine, my own breasts will start to grow. Okay?" He's talking to Jamie, but I know what he's saying is meant for me, too. I want to cover my ears so I don't hear.

"Okay," says Jamie. "You do look a bit funny, though. Your hair's all different. Can I touch it?"

"Yes, but don't mess it up," says Dad.

I turn my back on them to stir the bubbling pans of vegetables. They don't really need checking, but I need to do something. I don't want to hurt Dad's feelings, but I can't accept all these changes straightaway like Jamie seems to.

The doorbell rings. I can hear Mom opening the door and greeting Vicky. Dad goes out to join them in the hallway, and Jamie disappears back into the living room. There's a momble of adult voices. I decide to hide in the kitchen for as long as I can. I don't want to meet Vicky. I don't want to pretend that everything is normal.

But it seems there's no choice.

"... And this is our younger daughter Isabel," says Dad, as everyone squeezes into the tiny kitchen. "Hard at work over the stove." I smile weakly and nod hello. "Now let's get some water for those beautiful flowers."

I sneak a look at Vicky, while Mom and Dad fuss around looking for a vase. She's tall, with olive skin and black, bobbed hair. Probably a few years older than Mom and Dad. She's wearing fitted jeans, flat shoes, a bright blouse, with a deep blue scarf round her neck. She's carrying an enormous box of chocolates. You wouldn't look at her in the street and think she wasn't a woman. But then, I suppose, that's because she *is* a woman.

Vicky catches me looking at her, and says, "Hello, Isabel" softly, so I'm forced to say hello, too. Dad's right, you get the feeling that no one messes with Vicky.

We all go into the living room, where Vicky crouches down on the floor next to Jamie, who's got colored pens and paper everywhere. "I'm Vicky. You must be Jamie." Jamie nods. "Do you mind if I use some of your pens? What's your favorite animal?"

"Frog," says Jamie.

And Vicky starts drawing, with quick, skillful lines, and a frog appears. An actual, leaping, ribbiting frog.

Jamie is openmouthed, like SpongeBob SquarePants has stepped out of the TV into our living room. "Do a dog!" he demands. And she does. It has a panting tongue and its head on one side in an innocent, questioning look.

Mom whistles.

"I didn't know you could do that," says Dad appreciatively.

Vicky laughs a throaty laugh. "It's my misspent youth," she says. "All that doodling in exercise books and not

79

paying attention in class." And she winks at me. "Have you got a favorite animal, Isabel?"

I don't want to like Vicky. I really don't want to like her. But I think I do. She draws me the perfect cat, with legs outstretched, ready to leap.

By the time Megan comes down the stairs, and Dad jumps up and runs to the kitchen because he realizes the chicken's about to burn, there's a whole zoo spread across the floor.

Chapter Ten

Lunch is okay, too. The chicken's a bit tough, but not totally charred, and I still manage to have a third helping without Mom noticing. The conversation is not too dull, and Vicky tries to bring us all in, but without saying annoying things like, "I've heard so much about you," and, "Aren't you grown-up?" When she asks questions, she asks them like she actually wants to hear what you have to say. Even Megan starts talking to her about the gallery she runs and the artists she works with. Every couple of minutes Jamie interrupts with a new request for an animal drawing. Mom and Dad exchange smiles.

Once lunch is over, Vicky stands up.

"I know it's a filthy habit," she smiles, "but I'm dying for a smoke. Is it okay if I step out into the garden for a minute?"

"Yes, of course," says Dad.

"I'll put on a pot of coffee," says Mom. "Izzy, Megan, will you help clear up?"

"Actually, I wondered if Isabel might keep me company outside?" Vicky adds quickly, before I've even got up from my chair. "And I was hoping Megan wouldn't mind showing me some of her art later on, so perhaps she'll need a bit of time first to sort out her portfolio. . . ."

Mom raises her hands, smiling in mock-defeat. "All right, you two, you're off the chores—for now. Nice work, Vicky."

I think I'd rather scrape the dirty plates than be put on the spot by Vicky. I don't dislike her like I thought I would, but I don't feel comfortable with her either. I don't have a choice, though. She's done that thing that adults do, when it sounds like they're asking you to do something, but really they're telling you what's going to happen.

I quickly check my phone. Grace's posted loads of photos of her trying on different outfits and a message, which says: hope lunch not 2 awful, can I come round 2m after church for dvd? I pull on my jumper and follow Vicky out through the back door.

The garden is scattered with Jamie's toys. A few tomato plants are still struggling on and the garden furniture hasn't yet been packed under covers for the winter. Vicky leans against the garden table and lights up.

"Sorry, I am trying to give up, you know, but it hasn't worked yet." She pauses and blows the smoke away from me. I can feel her looking at me. "Not a very good influence, am I?"

I say nothing.

"It's okay, Isabel, I haven't brought you out here to interrogate you. I know I can be a bit much sometimes." She sighs. "It must be weird for you at the moment, like everything's changing. Your parents say you've been really understanding, but I bet there's plenty you're feeling angry or sad or unsure about, too. Maybe you just wish these last few weeks were a dream and you could wake up to life as you knew it before . . . and, above all, that there wasn't some big, brash woman you hardly know butting into your business."

I realize that this is what is so unsettling about Vicky. She sees right through you. She knows exactly what I'm thinking without me having to say anything.

"Tell me about you. I noticed your family call you 'Izzy' not 'Isabel.' Right? Do you like that better, or is it just for family? I don't want to call you the wrong thing!"

Normally, I don't like it when people I don't know very well call me Izzy. It feels like they're trying to make out they know me better than they do. It doesn't fit. And I hate it when people I don't like, like Mia, do it. But I know that asking Mia not to would make her do it even more. With Vicky, I don't know, but I like that she asked me, instead of just assuming. Grown-ups don't often do that.

"Izzy's fine," I tell her.

"Okay then, Izzy, what do you really love doing?" she asks seriously.

I wonder whether or not to tell her, and then I think, why not? She wouldn't laugh.

"I really like acting," I say. "People think I'm shy, but it's different being up onstage. I want people to look at me then."

Vicky laughs. "I'm the other way around. Everyone knows me as the loud and confident one, but put me in front of a room of people and I want to run and hide. That's why I like drawing. You do your showing off on paper—and people look at what you've made instead of at you! What do you love about getting up onstage?"

"Well, it's not so much being onstage," I say. "I don't

know, I like being part of a team, I suppose, fitting in, and I like imagining I'm someone else—moving like they'd move or speaking like they'd speak. And I like being good at something. I didn't think I would be, but I am." I feel myself blushing. "I'm not stupid, I don't think I'm going to be famous or anything, but I think I'll always want to act somewhere, somehow, even when I'm older."

"I heard you were in a show. *Guys and Dolls*, isn't it?" Vicky says and I nod. "I don't know much about musicals, I'm afraid."

Vicky looks out over the garden. She lowers her voice so that I have to lean in to catch what she's saying. "She's so proud of you, you know, not just the show, everything. She's always talking about you, your sister, and little Jamie. And your mom. You all mean the world to her. She would never want to hurt you."

At first, I don't know who Vicky's talking about. Then I realize that when she says "she," she means Dad. She says it so naturally.

But should I be listening to someone I've known five minutes telling me about Dad, who I've known all my life? How does she know what Dad really thinks and feels?

"What would you do if you couldn't act anymore, Izzy?" asks Vicky softly, cutting into my thoughts. It's another one of those questions where she expects an answer. She's not just asking to be polite, she really wants to know.

I think for a little while, trying to imagine if Mr. Thomas decided at school on Monday and said I couldn't be in the show, or in any show ever again. That I couldn't go to Drama Club or hang out with the people who did. That I couldn't even help with the lights or the programs or anything.

"It would be awful," I burst out. "Worse than anything, well, almost anything. I'd be miserable. Like a bit of me was missing."

"I know it's different," says Vicky thoughtfully, "but, in a way, that's a bit like how your dad's been feeling for years and years. Like a crucial part of herself is missing, because she hasn't been able to express who she really is. Now there's a chance for her to do that, to be that whole person."

I haven't thought about it like that. Is it my fault that Dad's been miserable inside so long? That he's been crying in the night? If he wasn't our dad, would he have been a whole other person, like Vicky says, much sooner? My head's been so full of what this means for me, I've hardly thought about what this is like for Dad, how hard it is for him. Suddenly I want Vicky to be quiet. I don't want to think about it anymore.

Since Vicky's asked me so many questions, I feel brave enough to ask her something in return. "How long have you been, you know, like this?" I stutter.

She smiles. "You mean how long since I transitioned?"

I nod.

"Oh, a long time, I had my last surgery more than ten years ago. I changed my name a few years before that. Like most trans people, I always knew, but it took a long, long time to get to where I am now. To be the person I really am, all the time, not just in secret. But it was harder back then, people were a lot less understanding."

We both stand in silence for a few moments. I can hear the whir of a mower a few gardens down, and the birds singing to each other.

"I guess you're worried that people, especially at school, won't be very understanding now either," she says, breaking the silence. "Maybe they will, maybe they won't," she continues. "But, from what your parents say about you, you're brave, Izzy. Getting up onstage in front of all those people, for a start, I could never do that. Whatever happens, you'll be okay."

"I just wish Mom and Dad weren't still saying they wanted to go and talk to the school," I blurt out. "It's not going to help anything. It'll just make things worse."

"Want to do it your own way? I don't blame you really. Though it's always good to have people watching your back. . . . Perhaps your teachers can—" She catches my stare. "Well . . . And Megan feels the same? Okay then. Do you want me to have a word? Maybe suggest they leave it a bit before talking to your school?"

"Yes, please, would you?"

"All right, but no promises." She sighs. "You're very lucky, you know. I see Danielle, and you all, even just for a few hours, and it's clear how much you care for each other."

She stubs out her cigarette and stands up. "Now, before I get all emotional, and that coffee gets cold, let's go back inside. I'm sure your mom has managed to keep a few chores waiting for you."

Chapter Eleven

It's Sunday afternoon and, as promised, Grace is ringing on the doorbell and dancing through the front door.

"Hi, Grace," says Mom, as she bounces into the kitchen. "We see you so much these days that we should really get you a key cut."

"Or perhaps just a little bed somewhere," suggests Grace chirpily. "I could curl up in a corner out of the way. I'd be less trouble than getting a dog. And more entertaining."

"Don't be silly," says Mom, smiling. "Anyway, you know you're always welcome here. You're like one of the family. And you don't eat us out of house and home like this one does," she says, nodding at me.

I'm starting to feel a bit left out of the double act that Mom and Grace seem to have got going. After all, Grace's *my* best friend, not Mom's. I'm about to drag her upstairs, when Dad comes into the kitchen.

There's a moment when it all goes quiet. I realize that he's styled his hair and is wearing his new clothes and I wonder what on earth Grace is going to think and say and do now. I bet Mom's thinking the same thing, for all of her Grace-is-part-of-the-family chat. I'm holding my breath. Will she freak out or will she pretend nothing's out of the ordinary?

"Hi, Mr. P," says Grace. "Like the outfit. Pretty good. Especially those shoes. Although, a word to the wise, that red lipstick's a bit last season. It's all deep colors now."

I breathe out.

Sometimes, like now, I cannot understand how Grace says the things she does to adults and gets away with it. But, like now, she nearly always does.

"Oh, hang on." Her hand shoots up to cover her mouth. "I can't really call you Mr. P anymore, can I?"

"About that," says Mom quickly. "Your whole Mrs. P and Mr. P thing. I don't know how it started, but it's probably time to let that go anyway. It always makes me feel a bit old, to be honest. How about you just call me Kathleen?"

"And you can call me Danielle," says Dad.

"Okay," agrees Grace and then she puts on her posh voice. "Now, Kathleen and Danielle, it's been very pleasant to see you, but Izzy and I have a few important things to discuss, please excuse us." Before I have a chance to say anything, she's swooped me out of the room and halfway up the stairs.

"Your dad," says Grace thoughtfully. "I told you he'd look all right."

"She," I interrupt.

"Oh, yeah." Grace smiles. "Wow, I suppose I should say 'she' now, shouldn't I? Bit of a shock, though—the new look. Is that it now then? New clothes, new name and everything?"

"Dunno. Guess it is." I shrug, calmer on the outside than I feel inside.

"Wow," says Grace again, shaking her head. "Things *are* getting more interesting in Littlehaven. You can't moan that your life's boring anymore, can you?"

"So, *do* we have important things to discuss?" I ask her, changing the subject.

"What? Oh, that. No, not really. I just thought it sounded mysterious," she replies.

We spend the whole afternoon chatting and laughing,

going over our lines, lying on my floor listening to music, Grace talking about Sam and me listening to her talk, until it's time for Grace—*Guys and Dolls* DVD in hand—to go home.

Shortly after Grace's gone, there's a soft knock on my bedroom door.

"Yeah?" I shout, expecting Mom or Dad, since Jamie doesn't knock, he just runs in.

"It's me," says Megan. "Can I come in?"

Megan and I used to play together all the time when we were little. We shared a room with bunk beds in our old house, before Jamie was born. Her on the top, me on the bottom. If I couldn't sleep or if I had a nightmare, she'd climb down, curl up in my bunk, and tell me stories. She used to tell me secret things that she wouldn't tell Mom and Dad, about boys she liked or teachers she hated or the time she skipped school just to see whether she'd get away with it. I think she liked trying to impress me. But she hasn't been in my room for months now, except I know that sometimes she sneaks in to take some of my socks if she's run out.

"Sure," I say, and she edges in, not really looking at me.

Then she starts wandering round my room, picking

things up absentmindedly and putting them down, pulling books off my shelf at random, flicking through, and shoving them back in again. It makes me crazy when people move my stuff around without asking, and I'm just about to snap at her to stop when Megan says, "Do you think he's going to change his mind?"

I know exactly what she's talking about. I don't answer straightaway. I want to say: Yes, I do, he's just teasing us, playing a not-very-funny dad joke, everything will be back to normal soon. But I can't.

"No, I wish, but it's not going to happen, is it?"

"I thought he would at first," sighs Megan. "If we all showed him how upset we were. But then everyone else seemed all right about it. Jamie doesn't really get it, Mom's gone all till-death-do-us-part and it doesn't look like anything bothers you, as long as nothing gets in the way of your stupid show."

"Shut up. That's not true." I feel stung. "But what's the point of shouting and screaming about it? It's not going to change anything, is it? It's just going to make all of us more miserable."

"Better than just letting this happen without Mom and Dad understanding. . . . Better than losing Dad," she hisses.

I'm shaking now, and words are coming out without

me thinking. "I'm not the one pushing him away. *You're* the one who's making Dad feel even worse, not me. Of course I don't want things to change. And it's you who's stupid if you think I do."

Megan's got her back to me. She picks up a snow globe on my chest of drawers, turns it over, and looks at the base. She shakes it, so that the little people inside are engulfed in a swirling cloud of white.

"Leave my things alone. Don't come in my room and mess with my stuff," I shout. And then I see Megan's shoulders moving. She's crying.

I feel awful. I don't care what she does with my things, not really. I just want her to be all right again.

"Oh, Megs, stop it, don't cry, I didn't mean to make you cry. I didn't mean any of it." I reach out for her, but she shakes me off. Instead, she slumps down on my bed, with her head in her hands.

She's making me cry, too. And before long we are both sniveling and hiccupping like a pair of babies. "Your nose has gone red," she says, looking up and trying to crack a smile.

"Your eyeliner's gone everywhere," I reply. "Here, I've got some tissues somewhere." I dig out a half-empty box of tissues from under my bed. We must both look as bad as each other.

"Do you really think it's like we're losing him?" I ask.

"I don't know," says Megan, dabbing at her black-rimmed eyes. "When he told us, I was just worried about what everyone was going to say, how people would laugh, and school would be awful. But now, well, it sounds stupid, but I'm worried he's not going to be Dad anymore. He already looks different and sounds different and has different friends. . . ."

"And a different name, remember?" I finish for her. "He told Grace this afternoon, about being Danielle now."

"Danielle . . ." says Megan thoughtfully. "And hearing Vicky call Dad 'she,' that was weird. I know Dad said we should, but it just sounds so strange every time I try it out in my head."

"I know. Same here. But I guess we have to try, don't we?"

"Yeah," replies Megan grudgingly. "We do."

"What did you and Vicky talk about anyway?" I ask. "You know, when she came up to see your pictures?"

"Oh, all sorts of things," says Megan vaguely, kicking off her shoes and stretching her legs out onto the bed. Then she stops, clearly thinking about whether or not to tell me more. "Vicky said that she couldn't tell me what to do or how to feel, but that there was no point in punishing Dad, because she was already punishing herself." Megan stops and smiles. "See, I can get it right! Anyway, Vicky said all that would happen was that I'd just end up making myself feel bad, too. I've been thinking about it since yesterday. I guess she's right about one thing. I do feel bad."

"Me, too," I say.

She sighs again. "I'm sorry about all that stuff I said earlier. There's no point in punishing you either, is there? I don't really think your show's stupid." She pauses. "Well, only a bit. So, what shall we do now?"

"There's one thing we need to do," I say. "We need to come up with a new name for *us* to call Dad. I thought 'Dad' would still be okay, but it's not, not really, except maybe inside my head. It feels wrong now. But we can't use Danielle either, that's even more weird."

Megan nods. "Okay then. We need to talk to Jamie, too." She jumps up. "I've got an idea, back in a minute." And I hear her making her way down the stairs to Mom's office.

She comes back quickly with Jamie riding delightedly on her back. "Come on, Izzy, we're giving Jamie his bath today. Let's get the water running. Mom was a little bit suspicious about why we were being so helpful . . . but she wasn't going to argue."

Jamie loves bath-time. He's normally in there for ages, bubbles everywhere, sailing boats and dunking animals and pretending to swim in the ocean. And then he loves running through the house afterward, leaving wet footprints and soggy towels everywhere.

The bath fills with water and foam, and Jamie's jumping up and down with excitement at all the attention. Megan tests the temperature and then he bounds in. "Your faces are a bit funny-looking," he says, sitting down as we both lean over the side. "Your eyes are all red."

"Don't be so goofy," says Megan in a mock-scary voice. "Or I'll wash you down the drain." Jamie squeals with delight.

"Look, Jamie," I say. "We've got something important to talk about without Mom and Dad here."

"Is it about Christmas?" says Jamie excitedly. "Is it about my birthday?"

"No, it's not about Christmas, or your birthday, they're not for ages and ages. It's about Dad. You know how, well . . ."

"How he's going to be a woman now?" interrupts Jamie helpfully.

"Yeah, that's right. Well, we need to decide what we're going to call Dad."

"Dad's not the right name for a woman, is it?" pitches in Megan.

"What about . . . Mommy?" says Jamie.

"Eurgh, no," says Megan. "Sorry, Jamie, good idea, but too babyish. Izzy and I are too grown-up for 'Mommy.'"

"And 'Mom' is no good, because we've already got a mom," I add.

"Mom One and Mom Two?" says Megan and makes a face to show that she's joking.

"Mom A and Mom B?" I respond. "Maybe not . . . This is hard."

"Mommy-Daddy?" says Jamie.

"It's a bit of a mouthful! Try saying that a few times in a row. Mommy-Daddy Mommy-Daddy Mommy-Daddy Daddy-Mommy . . ." says Megan, like a tongue twister, and we all burst out laughing. It's been a long time since the three of us have laughed like this all together.

"I know," I say, with sudden inspiration, when I can speak again without giggling. "What about 'Dee'?"

"D?" says Megan, raising her eyebrows.

"Yeah, Dee. Short for 'Danielle' *and* short for 'Dad.' Sounds like a girl's name. Not too much of a tongue twister." I feel rather pleased that I've thought of something so neat.

"Dee," says Megan slowly. "Hmmm, maybe you've got

it, Izzy. What do you think, Jamie?"

"I like Dee," shouts Jamie, smacking his hands into the bubbles, so that foam spurts into the air and bath-water splashes Megan and me.

Before long, there's a full-blown water fight going on, soaking the bathroom so that later on Mom will roll her eyes and ask us if we have been raised by wolves or born in a barn, or something like that. But I don't care, because I think maybe we might all be okay.

Chapter Twelve

t's been a couple of weeks since Megan, Jamie, and I came up with Dad's new name. When we told her, she loved it straightaway, and Mom's started using it, too. But I still have to think carefully before I say it, and whenever someone else calls her "Dee," it takes me a moment, just a moment, to realize they are talking about Dad.

I hear the front door slam, and Dee's voice drifts up the stairs, angry and upset. I've been in my room, trying on different outfits for tonight, and hoping Mom won't notice that I've eaten the last cookie.

"Jesus Christ, what a stupid, ignorant prig of a woman. . . ."

"All right, enough now, Dee," Mom cuts in. "Enough, I've heard it, I agree, but enough. The kids will hear."

I've been listening to them talking in the background, but now I want to properly eavesdrop. I move silently as near to the top of the stairs as I can without being noticed. What other secrets have they got that they're not telling us?

Dee puts on a different voice: "'It would be better if you kept a low profile around school for now, *Mr.* Palmer, very young children can get confused about these things, you know.' What nonsense. We've been part of that school for eleven years, since Megan was five, it's not like they don't know me there."

So they've been to see Mrs. Garvey, Jamie's teacher. Mrs. Garvey's been at Woodside, the grammar school, for ever. She used to be my kindergarten teacher, too, and Megan's. Jamie loves her, always chattering on about her, but now all I can think of is how much she's upset Dee.

"She's only worried about other parents, about complaints to the school," continues Mom

"You bet she should be worried about complaints. I'm all ready to make a complaint."

"And what good would that do? How would that help Jamie?" snaps Mom. "That's why we went in the first place, remember? To make it easier for Jamie."

Dee's voice drops, so I have to strain to hear it.

"Confused? If there'd been one single person who even talked about being trans when I was at school, if there'd been a trans parent or a trans teacher, or even—God forbid!—a trans person in a book we read in class, well, perhaps I wouldn't have hated myself quite so much for all these years."

"Think how long it took you, how long it took us, to get to this point," says Mom wearily. "And she's had, what, ten minutes? Give it time. Look, let's sit down and have some tea."

I wonder how long Mom knew before they told me and Megan and Jamie. I haven't really thought about it; I just assumed that it was nearly as much of a shock for her as for the rest of us. But maybe it wasn't, maybe she's known for ages. Perhaps that's why she seems so calm about all this.

I decide now's the time to come downstairs. Since Vicky came over two weeks ago, neither of them has said any more about going into St. Mary's to talk to our teachers. Megan's been more relaxed since then, too. Now she's even talking to Dee again—well—as much as Megan talks to any of us.

It sounds like it's gone pretty badly with Mrs. Garvey, so they're hardly likely to want to do it at St. Mary's. I'm glad. Then I feel rotten because that's like wanting them both to be unhappy.

I clatter down the stairs as loudly as I can, so that they don't think I've been listening in.

"Oh, hi, Izzy," says Mom, flustered. "How was school today? How's your homework coming along?"

"Okay, I suppose, I've done a bit. . . ."

"Give her a break, Kath," chips in Dee. "It's not even six on a Friday evening. She's got the whole weekend to do it."

"I just want her to get a good start on it, that's all. There's lots more this year than in sixth grade, isn't there, Izzy?"

"Well, maybe," I say. "But I did most of it earlier in the week, honestly. . . ."

"That's my girl, you've got a sensible head on your shoulders," says Dee, satisfied.

"Actually, Mom, I was wondering about something," I say, shifting from one foot to another. "I totally forgot, but is it okay if I go out to the movies tonight? It's Olivia's birthday, and there's a whole group going. Sheetal's mom says she can take me home. I could get the bus there, but . . ." I tail off, hoping Mom takes the hint.

"I'm really sorry, Izzy, I can't give you a lift tonight. I'm shattered after today. I've got to pick up Jamie from Tom's and then get dinner, and there's still some work I need to fit in later. I wish you'd given me a bit of warning. . . ."

"I'll take her," interrupts Dee. "It's no problem."

I stop and stare, then start stuttering, "Da— um, sorry, Dee, it's okay, don't worry, I bet you're tired, too. I can get the bus. Really I can. I don't need a lift."

"No," says Dee slowly, in a voice that won't be contradicted. "I said it's no problem. What time are you meeting them?"

"Seven, but . . ."

"All right then, okay to go at twenty to?" says Dee. "That's plenty of time for you to get ready, and me to get a cup of tea."

It's okay Dad being Dee around the house. And it's okay seeing her going off to work in the mornings. And it's okay when Grace is here, because she's cool with everything. I know at some point other people from school are going to know. But I don't want it to be tonight.

I can't say it to Dee. I don't want to even think it, but I'm embarrassed at the thought they might see me with her. It's always been so easy to talk to Dad, but now I haven't got a clue what to say.

I hope it'll be getting dark by the time we go, but when we step outside it's one of those perfect, crisp autumn evenings, low sun lighting the street, every detail sharp and clear. I try really hard not to look around to see whether anyone can see us, but I can't help glancing down the road even so. Dee catches me looking, but doesn't say anything.

I snap my seatbelt in and turn on the radio. Dee starts the car. The music's loud, but I can feel the silence even louder underneath.

"You look cute," says Dee after a while, turning the radio down a little. "That top really suits you, matches your eyes. I'm going to need someone to start giving me fashion advice before long. There are plenty of trans women who get really carried away and dress in all sorts of crazy clothes. Vicky's been great, helping me think through all these things. She says that I wouldn't have been able to believe some of the things she wore when she first came out."

She pauses. "What did you think of Vicky, Izzy? Really?"

"I liked her," I say. "Her drawings were amazing. But, well, she was a little bit scary, too."

Dee laughs. "I know. She's like the old wise woman of the group—although I'm sure she wouldn't like me saying old!—she's not afraid to say what she thinks about anything. I'm glad you liked her."

We both go silent again. I try to look like I'm listening intently to the radio ads for car repairs and insurance.

Then Dee says, "Look, I *know* you're going to be embarrassed about me. That's okay, that's what being twelve's about, being embarrassed by your parents. I spent most of my teenage years telling your nana and grandad what they could and couldn't wear or do, or say, because I was so terrified that they would make me look bad."

She glances over at me. "I just don't want you to be *more* embarrassed because of my gender. Whether I'm a man or a woman doesn't change how much I care about you. Everyone's different, aren't they? If they weren't, the world would be a very boring place."

I know that's all true, but what Dee doesn't seem to get is that Littlehaven's not the easiest place to be different. We're not in a children's book, where the zebras and the lions or whatever all learn to get along despite their differences. This is a small town, and I don't want to be known as "Isabel Palmer, the one whose dad had a sex change" for the rest of my school life.

"I know you and Megan don't want us to go into St. Mary's and talk to your teachers," continues Dee. "And if you really don't want us to, then we won't." I breathe a sigh of relief.

"I'm not going to hide who I am, I've done enough of that, though I am going to *try* and take things slowly. But if anyone says anything to you or gives you any trouble about me, I want to know, okay? I don't want you to keep things from us. You can always talk to me or your mom."

"Yeah, okay," I say quickly as we turn into the parking lot. "Look, you don't have to wait for me to go in. Why don't you just drop me by Nando's? I can walk over from there."

Dee smiles. "All right, taking it slowly then. I'm not going to embarrass you today. I'll wait and watch you from here, though. No one's going to see me, if that's what you're worried about."

"No, it's not that, it's . . ."

"Go on," she says. "It doesn't matter. You'll be late."

When I'm halfway across the lot, I turn back and wave. Dee lifts a hand slowly and waves back.

When I step into the cinema lobby, the lights are dazzling. It seems like the whole of Littlehaven is here this Friday night. It takes a while to spot Olivia, Sheetal, Charlotte, and a couple of others in a huddle by the snack stand. Grace is not there yet.

My heart sinks when I see that Mia's part of the group. She's flicking back her long perfect auburn hair and laughing with Olivia about something. She's been even more funny than usual with me and Grace since the parts for *Guys and Dolls* were announced.

I wonder if Olivia's only invited me because I'm friends

with Grace. I start to worry that the top Dad liked looks a bit childish. I wish Grace was here. Perhaps coming out tonight was a mistake after all.

"Hey, Izzy, over here," calls Sheetal, waving me over. I take a deep breath and join the others.

"Oh, hello, Izzy," says Mia, as I approach the group. "I didn't know *you* were coming. Where's your twin tonight? I thought you two were stuck together with superglue." And she laughs, a false high laugh. "Or has she got fed up with you?"

"Grace just messaged me," says Olivia, before I can answer. "She'll be here in a couple of minutes. There's some drama going on, but I'm not sure what it is."

"There's always drama with Grace," says Sheetal, raising her eyebrows. "I wonder what it will be this time."

"Happy birthday, Olivia," I say, and then I feel stupid for saying it, because I only just saw her at school and anyway it's not really her birthday till Sunday. But no one else seems to think it's stupid.

"Thanks," says Olivia. "I'm so excited. My mom and dad are getting me something really special. They won't say what it is, but I think it's going to be a kitten."

"How do you know?" asks Charlotte.

"I've just got that feeling," says Olivia, clapping her

hands together.

"Aaah, that will be so cute. I'm so jealous," gushes Mia. "What are you going to call it?"

"Mmm, I don't know, depends what it looks like, I suppose. . . ." says Olivia, tilting her head to one side. "Or maybe I could call it Sky, you know, like Sky in the show."

"Sky, that's such an adorable name. Or you could call it Tommy, after Mr. Thomas." Mia glances at me. "Although that's probably more likely to be the name *Izzy* would choose. Isn't it, Izzy?"

I just stare at her, puzzled.

"After all," she continues, "we know you like him. It's so obvious. I bet you've got his name written all over your books."

"I don't . . . that's not true. . . ." I stutter. I can feel myself going red, despite trying my hardest to stay cool. Everyone's looking at me now.

"Oh my god, oh my god, I'm so sorry." It's Grace running in, out of breath and hair flying. "How late am I? Have we missed everything?"

"No, Grace, it's fine, we've still got time," says Olivia. "What happened to you?" And everyone's looking at Grace instead of me as she launches into one of her long stories, involving cars breaking down and neighbors pushing, and her mom praying for a miracle right in the middle of the street. Grace's stories are always much funnier and more dramatic than anything that actually happens in real life. Probably her mom just had a little bit of trouble getting the car started. But, with each story Grace creates her very own show to star in.

I'm not really listening this time, though, I'm trying to work out why Mia's being like this. Mia's not listening either. She's shuffling and playing with her hair. I wonder if she's fed up that she's not the center of attention. She keeps glancing down admiringly at her sleek, brown boots and tapping her feet, so that it's hard not to keep looking at them, too.

"Oh, you've noticed my boots then, Izzy?" she asks suddenly. "What do you think of them? I just got them last week."

"Yeah, they're really nice," I say.

"Where did you get them?" asks Grace admiringly. Mia's glowing now that everyone's looking at her again.

"My dad bought them when he was in Italy for business actually," she says. "I think they must have cost hundreds of dollars. He only buys things that are really top quality. He says otherwise you're just wasting your money on cheap junk." She pauses and casts a scornful look at Grace's feet.

"Where did you get yours, Grace?"

"Oh, just down at the mall, a few Saturdays ago," says Grace cheerfully, refusing to be drawn into a competition.

"I don't mean to be rude, Grace, but you can tell they're not such good quality, can't you? Still, they're okay . . . considering. I suppose it's all your mom can afford, what with your dad . . . well, you know. . . ." She laughs her high-pitched, nothing-actually-funny laugh again.

I can tell Grace is about to snap that her dad not being around is none of Mia's business. I so don't want there to be a scene.

"I like your boots better, Grace," I say loyally. Mia makes a face. Then Olivia says, "Come on, girls, let's get some sweets."

We giggle and jostle as the lights go down and the trailers start. I've been wanting to see this film for ages. I love that feeling you get in movies of being totally absorbed in what's on the screen, so that everything outside seems to disappear. But now I just can't settle back and enjoy it. Perhaps I should have stayed at home after all, then at least I would have been well out of Mia's way.

Grace reaches for a handful of popcorn with one hand and squeezes my arm with the other. "Don't let meanie

Mia get to you," she whispers.

"She's been like this all evening," I whisper back. "Before you got here she—"

"She's not worth it," interrupts Grace. "She's still jealous about not getting such a good part in the show. Just ignore her, there are far better things to think about."

So I decide that I will. I might not be as sure of myself as Grace, but I'm not going to let Mia, or anyone, spoil things tonight.

Chapter Thirteen

Something's changed.

I feel it as soon as I get into school on Monday morning, but I can't work out what's different.

The last few weeks have been so busy, filled with rehearsals and homework, that I haven't had much time to think. But it's felt like gradually, week by week, things at home have returned to normal. Well, not exactly the same normal that they were before, but a new, slightly-awkward-but-mostly-okay, kind of normal. A normal that works, as long as no one says anything.

Mom works for herself, so it's not like she gets proper holidays, but she took some days off at winter break—and spent them with us, without even checking her emails every five minutes—and so did Dee. Vicky came over a couple of times, too, and, even since the break, sometimes when I've got home late from rehearsal, I've found her and Megan chatting in the kitchen, even if Megan still barely talks to any of us. Maybe this is a sign that Megan's approaching a "normal human being" phase. I hope so.

At school, Grace is still pursuing Sam, of course, and obsessing over any little sign that he might possibly like her. I've been keeping out of Mia's way since that night at the movies.

Now, all of a sudden, November's here. It feels like winter—and the show—is just around the corner.

It's just before first period on Monday morning and I'm late.

I go through the contents of my bag and my locker three times, piling it all on the floor, shaking everything out, but *still* can't find my math book. Eventually I realize that just having no book is better than having no book *and* being late, and dash down the corridor to the math room. I hope the lesson hasn't already started. I hope someone is willing to share.

The lesson *has* already started.

"Thank you for joining us, Isabel," Mrs. Dalton says sharply, as I try to slip in without being noticed.

"Sorry, Mrs. Dalton," I mumble.

"Find yourself a seat then and don't waste any more of our time."

I glance around the classroom and my heart sinks: The only free seat is next to Lucas. We've been seeing each other a lot at rehearsals, but that doesn't mean I want to sit next to him in class as well. He's surprisingly good as Nathan, but as soon as he's offstage, it's the same stupid jokes and comments as ever. As I reluctantly slide in next to him, Lucas's hand shoots in the air.

"Mrs. Dalton, I can't sit next to *her*."

Everyone is looking at me. Charlie nudges Amir and they both laugh. I feel myself go red and bite my lip hard.

"Don't be ridiculous, Lucas," retorts Mrs. Dalton, looking round the class sternly. "And, everyone else, back to your work."

Lucas pushes his books and pens across the desk as far away from me as possible and shuffles his chair sideways so it's right up against the wall.

I don't know which is worse—telling Mrs. Dalton I haven't got my book or asking Lucas to share.

"I can't find my book," I whisper finally. "Can I share yours? Please."

Loud enough for most of the people around us to hear, Lucas whispers back, "No way . . . it might be catching."

"Isabel, Lucas, stop talking," says Mrs. Dalton, prompting more sniggers. "Isabel, this isn't like you."

"I'm sorry, Mrs. Dalton," I stutter. "I couldn't find my book this morning, and . . ."

"Isabel, I would expect you to be less careless. You are normally much more organized."

By the time Mrs. Dalton finds me a battered spare copy, my eyes are stinging with the unfairness of it all. The numbers on the page are swimming, as I struggle to hold back my tears. I don't want to be a baby, crying over something so stupid.

If Grace were here she'd make a face or crack a smile to cheer me up, but she's in a different group for math.

The lesson seems to go on for hours. I can't concentrate on any of the questions, with Lucas treating me like I've got the plague, turning around and smirking at Charlie and Amir all the time. I keep making mistakes and tying myself in knots.

Finally the bell goes. Lucas is off like a shot and I can't wait to get out. I return the book to Mrs. Dalton, who gives me another little lecture about looking after school property.

Hanging round outside the classroom is a small group of girls. There's Olivia, and then Sheetal and Charlotte.

We've all got history together next, so I guess they've waited for me. I smile gratefully, even though I don't really feel like talking to anyone right now.

"Hey, Izzy," says Olivia, linking her arm through mine. "Mrs. Dalton was so unfair today. She was in a foul mood even before you arrived. And Lucas, what a jerk."

"Thanks for waiting," I say. "It's been a nightmare this morning. Everyone seems in a weird mood today, not just Mrs. Dalton. What's up?"

There's a silence. Sheetal, Charlotte, and Olivia all look at each other, as if waiting to see which of them is brave enough to speak first.

"Come on, what is it?"

"We-ell," says Olivia slowly. "We heard about your dad. . . ."

She pauses and leaves the words hanging there, before Charlotte starts talking.

"We want you to know that we don't think there's anything wrong with it, like, we don't think it's disgusting or anything."

"Charlotte!" hisses Olivia, trying to shut her up.

"I mean, it must be weird for you, but, you know, people should be whoever they want to be, right?"

I nod weakly. What do they mean they've heard about

my dad? How? When? Who from?

"I think it's cool," adds Sheetal. "Like you can go clothes shopping with your mom *or* your dad."

"I wouldn't go shopping with *my* mom," grimaces Olivia, and pushes open the door to the history classroom. "She hasn't got a clue."

We're the last ones in. I've only just avoided being late again, but luckily Grace is there first and has saved me a seat. She's desperate to talk, but I don't know what to say. Only now that I've sat down does my brain start to process what Olivia and Charlotte were saying. They know about Dad. They *know*. But how?

Grace is wondering the same thing. "Everyone's talking about Dee," she whispers. "How do they know? I've had loads of people asking me if it's true."

"What did you say?" I whisper back, forcing the words out. A cold feeling is creeping over me, slowly spreading through my whole body. I can't help shivering. So this is it now. Everybody knows. Nothing will be the same again. Grace gives me a worried look and squeezes my hand.

"I didn't say anything, of course. I didn't know what you'd said already. Why can't people just mind their own business?"

Grace stays by my side most of the day, helping fend off questions and staring down anyone who looks like they are about to say anything.

By the time the final bell rings, I'm exhausted. But I can't go home yet.

Chapter Fourteen

I'm rummaging in my locker for my script when something catches my eye. It's the corner of my math book, sticking out from under the lockers. I grab it with relief, before spotting the red pen scrawled across the cover: IZZYS DADS A PERV.

I shove the book deep into the bottom of my bag, feeling sick. I want to run home and hide, but I can't miss rehearsal. It's the one thing I've been looking forward to all day.

However, the thought of standing up in front of people, singing my heart out, makes my throat feel dry and my legs start to tremble. I only make it because Grace comes to find me and marches me off to the studio, arm in mine. "Just get through today," she instructs me. "Everyone will be talking about something else tomorrow."

Yeah, right.

When we get to the studio, most of the others are gathered around the costume rail. I slide into the room as quietly as possible. Grace knows that I don't want to be noticed today, so she doesn't do her usual grand entrance.

Lucas is parading up and down, simpering, with one of the dancer's pink feather boas wrapped round his neck.

"Look at me, I'm Izzy's dad, don't I look pretty?" I hear him say as he waves the boa around, and flutters his eyelashes. "Just picking up a few fashion tips from my little girl Izzy..." Mia's leaning on the end of the rail, flicking her hair, laughing, and saying, "No, Lucas, don't, stop it, it's too much," in a high-pitched, giggly voice.

Then she looks up and catches my eye, and holds it for a couple of seconds, looking very satisfied with herself. Finally, she looks away and hisses, "Lucas," nodding her head in our direction.

Lucas stops short. Once they notice me, people start to shuffle away, embarrassed, and start up their own conversations. But most are still casting sideways glances over at us, eager to see what's going to happen next.

Lucas doesn't look embarrassed, though, he just laughs.

"Grow up, Lucas," calls out Grace. "If *you* want to wear pink, you just go ahead. I'm not sure how much it suits you, though. But just shut up and leave other people alone."

A few people giggle and a couple of others give Grace a little cheer. Before Lucas has the chance to reply, Mr. Thomas comes in, and claps his hands to get us started.

"He's only messing around to impress moaning Mia," whispers Grace, as we all get into our places for today's scene. "Although why she'd fancy him, I don't know. I guess they are pretty well suited. Just as stupid as each other."

For a split second I feel bad for listening to Grace being mean about Mia and Lucas. Until I remember the triumphant expression in Mia's eyes—she was enjoying every moment—and the genuine disgust on Lucas's face when he had to sit next to me during math this morning.

Everyone settles down and rehearsal starts. We all know there are only three weeks to go, and so much still to get through. Even Lucas doesn't want to screw it up and look stupid onstage in front of everyone.

I'm not going to let Lucas and Mia spoil this for me. Not just the performance itself, but how I feel being part of the cast, when we're all united and supporting each other. It's the best thing ever. So I try my hardest to stay focused.

Unfortunately rehearsal turns out to be just like everything else today. I can't concentrate. I get all my lines wrong and stumble over the words. I even manage to turn the wrong way in one of the dances and crash right into Sam, which makes everyone laugh. The magic spell that seems to banish all my shyness when I step on the stage has lost its power today.

"All right then," shouts Mr. Thomas. "It's a wrap. We're done for today. Well done. You've all been working hard, but perhaps some of you need a bit of a rest." I know he's looking at me. "Next time let's try and keep focused, and do your best to get those lines learned. Tickets go on sale this week, so make sure your families know all about it. We're going to have a great show for them. And, last thing, if anyone can give me a hand over tomorrow lunchtime to fold hundreds of programs, I'd be extremely grateful."

Noise levels soar. There's a scramble to grab bags and coats and to get out of the door. I move slowly, head down, reluctant to meet anyone's eyes, still trying not to be noticed.

As Grace and I are on our way out, arm in arm, Mr. Thomas calls her back.

"Grace, can you wait a couple of minutes? I just need a quick word about your English assignment."

"But, Mr. Thomas—" says Grace.

"But nothing. It won't take long." He sees me standing

there, too, and waves me away with his hand. "Go on, Isabel, you can wait outside. Honestly, you two, you can survive apart for five minutes, you know. . . ."

There's a low wall alongside the bike sheds. It's sheltered from the wind, but Grace will be able to spot me when she comes out of the studio so we can still walk home together. I sit down, hood up, earphones on, blocked off from the world. I just want today to be over.

I must have drifted off into my own thoughts because I jump out of my skin when I feel a light touch on my arm.

"Sorry, I didn't mean to scare you," says Sam, as he sits down beside me on the wall. "Okay if I wait here?"

I shrug and turn off my music. We sit in silence for a bit. Sam opens a packet of potato chips.

"Want some?" he says, and I take a couple. His knees are jiggling up and down and he looks nervous. In fact, this is probably the first time I've seen Sam look anything less than cool. We haven't really exchanged more than a few words, apart from those in the script, since that very first rehearsal.

"Izzy," he says finally.

"If it's about me falling into you earlier," I say. "I'm really sorry."

Sam shakes his head. "No, it's not that. It's about your dad."

Oh, no, he's going to say something. Even if it's the most caring and supportive and understanding thing in the world, I don't want anyone to say anything, not even Sam Kenner. I just want them all to leave me alone. Forever.

"About your dad..." he repeats and then seems to get stuck.

"It's, well, it's, I'm not sure if I...look, it's just that...my dad's like your dad."

"What?" My head snaps up from under my hood. "Your dad's nothing like my dad."

I've only seen Sam's dad once or twice, when he's come to pick him up after Drama Club. I can't really remember what he looks like, but a picture swims into my mind of a serious-looking man with a neat beard, sitting in the car reading the paper.

There's no way he's like my dad. I can't see him with a pair of pink high heels hidden at the back of the closet or putting on makeup in front of the bathroom mirror. I don't understand why Sam is messing about like this. He's not one of those boys who usually plays stupid jokes.

"You mustn't tell anyone," he says seriously. "But my dad used to be a girl. I'm not winding you up, I wouldn't do that. Swear to god, it's true."

I can't quite take it in. "Why should I believe you?"

"Why would I make this up?"

"But how did you find out?" I ask.

"I didn't, I mean, obviously I do know, but I don't remember ever *not* knowing," says Sam quietly. "My dad transitioned before I was born, see, before he even met my mom. I've always known. When I was a kid, they'd tell me things like how people used to think Daddy was a girl when he was little, but he always knew he was a boy. Stuff like that. They always wanted me and my brother to know. Now they don't talk about it so much, unless I ask. Except to say that it's nothing to be ashamed of. But I always used to wonder, if they're not ashamed, and we're not to be ashamed, why is it such a big secret?"

"Yeah, my mom and dad say that, too, about this being nothing to be ashamed of." I swallow nervously. "But I can't help feeling embarrassed, you know? I didn't want anyone at school to know. I hate it now they do. It's no one else's business." My eyes are stinging again, as I remember the looks and the whispers.

"I think that's how my dad feels, too," agrees Sam. "That it's no one's business but his."

He takes the potato chip bag and smooths it out on his knee, folding it into a tiny perfect triangle. I've always been impressed by people who can do this. Whenever I try, I just make a crumpled mess. As we're both looking at the packet, Sam starts talking again, even more quietly this time.

"A couple of years ago, I got my gran to show me some baby photos, from when Dad was a girl. She told me what it was like when he was a kid. He had such a hard time at school for being different. In the end, he dropped out without graduating."

"That's awful," I gasp.

"Even my gran and grandad didn't understand. They kept trying to send him for different therapies and things. But it didn't change anything. I guess that's why he doesn't want to talk about it now. He's had enough of the hassle—and doesn't want us to get any hassle either, because of him."

Listening to Sam, I have a terrible, sickening thought. "So what happened to your dad at school?" I ask.

"He got called names, ignored, spat at, one time he got beaten up so bad he could hardly open his eyes they were so swollen. That's what my gran said. Dad won't talk about it."

I think for a moment. "Do you think stuff like that will happen to my dad, too?"

Sam shrugs. "I don't think so, that was years and years ago, wasn't it?"

127

I'm not sure if he means it, or if he's just trying to make me feel better.

He leans toward me, looking totally serious. "If you ever want to talk, about your dad, or anything, you can talk to me. But you mustn't tell anyone about my dad, Izzy, you mustn't. Not even Grace, not your dad, not anyone. If my parents know I've told, they'll be really angry." He corrects himself, "No, not angry, disappointed. That's probably worse."

Sam reaches over and puts his hand on mine. "Promise?"

"Promise," I say.

When I look up, there's Grace, standing still as stone, looking right at us. She's got an expression I've never seen on her before. Angry and sad and shocked all at once. I drop Sam's hand like it's burning hot.

Grace turns around and starts running. I jump up, grab my bag, and run after her.

"Izzy!" says Sam. "Do you want me to—"

"No," I call over my shoulder. "No, I'm fine, it's fine."

She's halfway down the road by the time I catch up with her. I've always been faster than her, but now we're both panting and out of breath.

"Grace . . . Grace . . . please stop, please listen," I plead. She turns her back and keeps walking.

"I don't want to talk to you," she says in a choked voice.

"Go away."

"It's not what you think," I say.

"Oh, really?" she snaps, spinning around to face me. "Really? So I didn't see you holding hands with Sam Kenner, staring into his eyes, whispering to him? That was all my imagination, was it? Come on. What's going on, Izzy?"

"Nothing's going on, I promise. Stop being such a drama queen. We were just . . . talking."

"Oh yes, and what were you 'talking' about?"

I realize that I can't tell her. For the first time in my life, I have to keep a secret from Grace. She's always the one I tell about what worries or scares me, about when something really embarrassing happens or what's going on in my family. I don't think I've even tried to keep something from her before.

"I can't tell you, Grace, I can't," I stutter, knowing how pathetic that sounds. "I'm sorry."

Her face falls. Like this was a test. The only thing I had to do was tell her the truth—and I failed.

"I promise you, there's nothing going on with me and Sam. You've got to trust me."

"Why? Why should I trust you? You're my best friend. You *know* how much I like him, you know more than anyone else does. I bet you've been laughing at me with him. 'Oh, look how stupid Grace is for not knowing what's going on.'"

I'm starting to lose patience. I know Grace's upset, but I've had the day from hell and she's not even trying to listen.

"I don't know if I can trust you either," I snap. "How did everyone find out about Dad unless you told them? You were the only one who knew."

As soon as I say it, I want to claw the words back. I know Grace would never have told. It was a stupid, stupid thing to say. I feel even worse when I see Grace's face, she looks like someone's punched her and she's struggling to breathe.

"You know what, Izzy, I would never, ever betray your secrets," she says slowly. Then in a rush come the words to hurt me like I must have just hurt her. "Maybe Pastor Johnson's right after all about families like yours."

"What do you mean?"

"People like your dad. He says they're not normal. They're sick. Pastor says it's an abomination for men to dress like women. It's in the Bible."

Everything suddenly feels very far away. All I can hear is my own heart beating.

Grace carries on walking. This time I don't try to run after her.

Chapter Fifteen

I'm not sure how long it is before I move. Before I notice that I'm shivering, and that it's getting dark. I can see that the streetlights are on, and I know that Mom and Dad will be expecting me home. Even so, it's a struggle to move my feet. I don't know if I can face them. Maybe if I just don't think about this . . .

I let myself in and wince at how bright and loud the house is. The curtains are drawn against the night and all the lights are blazing. The TV is on full blast, and Mom is singing to herself in the kitchen. Jamie runs up and demands I play with him.

"Sorry, Jamie, not right now," I say, surprised that my voice comes out sounding almost normal.

"That was a long rehearsal," says Mom as she comes out

of the kitchen. She gives me a peck on the cheek. "Go on, don't just stand there, take your coat off, we're about to eat."

"Actually, Mom, I'm not feeling that hungry," I say quietly. "I think I might just go to my room and lie down if that's okay."

Mom turns back. She puts her hand under my chin, and pushes it up gently so that she can look me in the eye. I notice we're almost the same height. I can't hold her gaze for long.

"Are you okay?" she asks softly. "It's not like you not to want to eat."

"I'm fine, just a bit tired, and there's this bug going around at school, so I think I'll just . . ."

"Nothing bad's happened, has it?" she interrupts.

I shake my head, not quite trusting myself to speak.

Thankfully, Jamie runs out and wraps himself round Mom's knees. "Mommy, I'm hungry. I'm so hungry I'm going to explode into a million, billion pieces—and Izzy won't even play with me," he moans.

"Keep yourself together, Jamie, we're just about to eat. Okay then, Izzy, get yourself to bed. I'll bring you up something in a bit—or come down if you feel better." She continues, "I wonder if you girls all do too much, perhaps sometimes you should just slow it down a bit, concentrate on your schoolwork, not all this extra stuff."

I lie down on my bed. I feel like there's no space left in my head. The comments from Lucas, the conversation with Sam, the argument with Grace—it's all too much for one day.

I pull on my pajamas, and get out my phone in case Grace calls. I put it on the bedside table, close at hand.

I wonder about texting her. I pick up the phone. Then put it down again. Then pick it up. I want to . . . but what would I say? After what she said, she should be the one to apologize to me.

I pull out the crumpled piece of paper from under the corner of the mattress and smooth it out on my lap. I read again where Grace has written, *SUPERSTAR. BEST FRIENDS FOREVER*, and then I start to slowly scrunch up the paper in my fist. When it's in a tight little ball, I spread it out again and rip the page from top to bottom. I rip and rip and rip until there's nothing but tiny shreds of paper on my bedroom floor. No pink hearts, no tiny stars. All gone.

That word keeps pounding in my head: *abomination, abomination, abomination*. Each time like a bomb going off.

The next thing I hear is someone gently closing the door behind them as they slip into my room. My mouth feels dry and my legs heavy. I must have fallen asleep on top of the covers.

I jolt awake, and grab my phone to see if there's anything from Grace.

No new messages.

"Sorry, I didn't realize you were asleep," says Dee softly. "You don't have to sit up. I just brought you a hot chocolate." She sits on the edge of the bed. "I wanted to see if you were all right."

I smile gratefully and wrap my hands around the warm mug.

After a while, she says, "If there's anything you want to talk or ask about, I'm here to listen."

I shake my head, as if the movement itself could sort out all the jumbled events of the day into an order that makes sense.

I think of what Sam said about his dad, about all the hassle he suffered growing up. I don't want Dee to go through anything like that. She doesn't have to know about today. She shouldn't have to worry about me, too.

As if reading my mind, she says, "You don't have to protect me, you know."

But I do, I think.

The air is full of all the words not being said.

Dee waits a bit longer, squeezes my hand, and then stands up.

"You're a good girl, Izzy, but you don't have to be perfect. Get your rest. I hope you feel better in the morning."

I know suddenly that I don't want her to go. I don't want to be left alone.

"Da— uh, Dee . . . ?"

"Yes."

"Will you . . . will you read to me?"

It must be years since I've been read aloud to. Dad used to read to Megan and me all the time when we were little, especially when we were ill. Whenever I walk past Jamie's room and overhear Dee's voice reading him a bedtime story, I feel kind of jealous, even though I know I'm much too old for bedtime stories.

Dee looks surprised. "Of course, go on, snuggle under the duvet. Anything in particular—or shall I find something on the shelf?"

"Whatever you like," I say, curling up in bed. I feel unbelievably tired.

Dee starts to read, stroking my hair gently. It's *Alice in Wonderland*, but I'm so sleepy that the last thing I hear is when she starts falling, falling, falling down the rabbit hole into the unknown.

Chapter Sixteen

"Are you sure you're well enough to go in?" says Mom, looking at me with concern. "You still look white as a sheet."

"She's just pretending," says Megan scornfully. "She's probably got a math test or something and doesn't want to go in. You shouldn't let her get away with it."

"Megan," Mom says sharply. "It's not up to you. You're not the boss here."

"Just telling it like it is," Megan replies. "As you're too blind to see it."

"I do feel a bit under the weather," I say. I know I can't hide under the duvet forever, but it can't really be lying when the thought of going back into school today does make me feel genuinely ill.

"I've got a lot of work to get done," says Mom thoughtfully. "There's the payment system for that restaurant chain site due tomorrow, but if you can just look after yourself for the morning, then I reckon I could have a break and we could have lunch together. That would be nice. You could get some homework done, too— if you feel up to it, of course."

"Faker," whispers Megan, and she swings out of the door, pretending to be sick behind Mom's back.

"I'll call the school. Oh, but Grace will be here any minute, won't she? Can she pass the message on that you won't be in, do you think?"

I panic. I can't imagine that Grace will be here any minute. She didn't text me all last night, or this morning. Even if she was coming, what would we say?

"I don't think she'd be allowed, Mom. It has to be an adult," I fib. "Anyway, I know she wasn't feeling very well yesterday either, so probably she's got it, too. I don't think she'll be in today."

I'm right, Grace doesn't knock for me. Of course she doesn't. I spend the morning on the sofa, wrapped in a duvet, watching TV, and wondering what's happening at school.

"Here, move over," says Mom. She's come through

from the kitchen with a cup of coffee in one hand and a large brown envelope in the other. Her glasses are pushed up onto the top of her head. "Is there room for me on the sofa, too? I need a break, I'm starting to get square-eyed staring at that screen."

It's not usually just the two of us, so it feels a bit odd at first. I hope she's not going to ask me about homework, or whether anything's wrong at school.

When I move over, she flops down next to me with a sigh. "I knew I had these somewhere, and now I've found them," she says, opening the envelope and tipping a bundle of old photos into my lap. "Have a look."

I flick through the photos. They are a bit tatty, some with little holes at the top or faded corners, like they've been pinned up on a noticeboard for a long time. Some of the people look familiar, but it takes me a moment to work out who they are: These are old photos of Mom and Dad.

"It's you! Wow, what *have* you done to your hair? And you're smoking!" I exclaim.

Mom's smiling in the photo, a cigarette poking out between red-lipsticked lips, a low, scoop-necked top and an enormous pile of black hair on her head.

"It's not my hair, you dope, it's a wig," she says. "That's

when we were in *Grease* in sixth grade. The cigarette's a prop. I wasn't really smoking."

"And what about this one? You look just like Megan here."

Mom puts her glasses on to look more closely at the picture. "Really?" she says. "I suppose maybe a bit. That's the whole cast, look, there's Dee, in the row behind."

They all look so happy, so young. "It's so long ago," I say. "It must be, like, twenty years."

"More than that," says Mom. She pauses, then, "You see now why we're not splitting up, don't you? That you don't have to worry about any of that."

It's not enough.

"Just because you've been together a long time doesn't mean . . . I mean, everything's changed now, hasn't it?"

"Has it? Really? I mean, yes, of course, in some ways this is a huge change for us all to get used to. Chloe thinks I'm a fool for putting up with it."

"Chloe?" I say, suddenly angry. "What's it got to do with her? When did you talk to her?" Did Mom's best friend know before we did? I wonder.

"Hey, steady. We talked about it on Skype the other night. Chloe cares about me. She's my oldest friend. You talk to Grace about what's going on, don't you? Same with me and Chloe—just not for every second of every day like you two!"

"It's still none of her business," I say sulkily.

"Maybe, maybe not. I love her dearly, I do, and I wish she didn't live on the other side of the world so you could get to know her a bit better. But there are a few things she doesn't understand. She doesn't have children, for one, and she hasn't been living with Dee for all these years."

I carry on looking through the photos, not meeting her eye.

"Izzy, you know you said everything had changed?" I nod. Mom continues, "Well, for me, only one thing's changed. Just one, and that's why we're not keeping secrets anymore. I know it's hard, sweetheart, but that's all that matters."

She pushes herself to her feet and drains her cup. It's awkward again, like she's embarrassed about having said too much. "I'd better get back to work now. Do you want anything else first—a drink? Something to eat?" She adjusts the duvet around me.

I shake my head. "Just, can I keep this photo?" I hold up one of Mom and Dad, not in costume, but still making funny faces at the camera.

"Of course. It's yours." She peers more closely. "Do you know what? I do look like someone else in that photo, and it's not Megan. I think I look like you."

Chapter Seventeen

Despite the lack of nagging from Mom, I do get some homework done in the afternoon. By the time Mom goes to pick up Jamie, and Megan comes in from school, I've finished my history and I'm halfway through the English. I've checked my phone about a hundred times. Grace hasn't messaged me.

"Goody Two-shoes!" says Megan. "The whole point of playing sick is to *avoid* doing work, not to sit at home catching up on your essays."

I scowl at her.

The doorbell rings. My stomach turns over.

"Megan, can you go?" calls Mom. "My hands are full, and it might be the Amazon packages."

"Can't Izzy get it?"

"No, you know she's not well. Go on."

Megan grudgingly moves toward the door as slowly as possible. There's some murmuring, and then she's back at top speed.

"Izzy, it's for you . . . and it's a boy." She raises her eyebrows. "Not a bad-looking one either. Very tall. How come you didn't tell your one and only beloved big sister that you have a boyfriend?"

"Because I don't!" I snap, running my fingers through my greasy, slept-on hair. "Can't you tell whoever it is that I'm sick?"

"Nope," sings Megan jubilantly. "Too late. I said you were on your way. Anyway, you look gorgeous! Nice pink pajamas!" She laughs. "Don't keep him waiting on the doorstep now."

I throw on my robe and shuffle to the door.

Waiting outside is Sam Kenner.

He's regained his cool overnight. He doesn't look anything like he did yesterday, when he told me his secret. He's standing on the doorstep like he belongs there, looking unruffled. He doesn't even seem to notice my ratty old robe.

"Hi, Izzy," he says, smiling his slow smile. "You all right?"

"What are you doing here?" I ask. "How do you even know where I live?" A thought strikes me. "You didn't ask Grace, did you?" If it was possible to make things any worse, Sam asking Grace for personal information about me would do it.

"No, I asked Olivia if you were in school today. She told me you were out sick, so I asked her for your address. I knew it wouldn't be far, as you don't take the bus in."

He shifts from foot to foot. "I just wondered if you were all right, after yesterday. It looked like things weren't so good with you and Grace, and when I saw her today without you, well, the two of you are always together. Then I heard you were home. Even Mr. Thomas was asking if you were okay."

"It's freezing with the door open," shouts Mom. "Is it Grace? Ask her in—and shut that wretched door."

"I'd better go, it's cold," I say quickly. "I'm fine. Don't worry about me." I can see my smile hasn't quite reassured Sam. In the last twenty-four hours I've felt less fine than I've felt in my whole life, yet that's all I seem to be able to say to anyone: *I'm fine, I'm fine, I'm fine.*

"See you tomorrow then, Izzy?"

"Yeah, see you tomorrow." He turns to go.

"And, Sam—"

"Yeah?"

"Thanks for coming over."

He nods, raises a hand, and disappears into the dark.

Chapter Eighteen

"Haven't you left yet?" asks Megan, mouth full of toast, shoving plates in the dishwasher.

"Doesn't look like it, does it? Last time I checked, I was still here," I snap back and carry on pushing my Corn Flakes into a mushy pile in the corner of my bowl. I'd woken up with a hard, tight knot in my stomach.

I don't want to go into school today. I don't want to face Lucas with his stupid comments, or Olivia with her nosy questions, or even Sam, now that I'm carrying his secret for him, too. Most of all, I don't want to face Grace.

It's already ten minutes after she'd normally knock for me. If I don't leave soon, I'll definitely be late. She's not going to come. But I can't bring myself to move. I want to keep waiting. Just in case.

Mom's voice breaks into my dream. "*Both* of you, you need to go. Now. Have you seen the time? If Grace's this late, she's going to have to get there on her own. Go on, out." And she shoos us out of the door with a quick kiss.

"Come on then," says Megan, once we're on the street. "Looks like you're walking to school with me today, little sister." She strides off, and I scuttle behind her.

Megan and I never walk to school together. I've always thought it was because she didn't want to be embarrassed, dragging around her baby sister. But maybe it's not that at all. Maybe it's just that I've always been too busy with Grace.

"Okay," she says, pulling out her earphones and leaving them dangling round her neck. "So, what's up with you and Grace? She's not really running late, is she?"

I shrug.

"Have you two had a falling out?"

I keep on walking with my head down, pretending there's something really interesting on the pavement in front of me.

"You have, haven't you?" She's quiet for a moment. "Oh, god, Izzy, it's not about that boy, is it? That tall one. Sam, is it? You haven't fallen out with Grace over a *boy*?" She shakes her head and puts on her concerned look. "It's not worth it, it's really not. You know that, don't you?"

Megan likes to sound all grown-up, like she knows everything there is to know about relationships. It's not even like she's had loads of boyfriends. She's really annoying me right now, even though I know she's trying to be nice. Nice in her own, super-annoying way. But, I suppose, if Grace isn't going to be my friend anymore, Megan's all I've got.

I want to tell her what happened with Grace, but instead I find myself blurting out: "Someone in my class found out about Dee and now everyone knows. It's been horrible. I didn't want to tell you, because you don't want anyone to know and you might think it's all my fault that they do, but it's not. . . ."

"Hey, slow down. It's okay. I've not been keeping up with what's going on in seventh grade." She sighs. "Look, I should have told you before. I've been doing a lot of thinking and reading—Mom gave me this list of websites. . . ."

"Oh, yeah, she gave them to me, too."

"And, well," she carries on, "I reckon, this is how it is now, isn't it? We've got to get used to it. So, I talked to a few people in my art class about Dee, and her transition . . ."

This is the first time I've heard Megan use that word: transition.

"I didn't know what they'd say, but actually most people think it's pretty cool. A couple of the boys were a bit weird, making jokes and stuff, but that's all. And then Ms. Maltoni told us all about Grayson Perry, who's this really amazing artist, although he's a transvestite and not transgender, and I had to tell her there's a big difference there. I mean, being transgender isn't just about the clothes you wear, is it? It's about who you are."

"*Is* that the difference?" I ask. I don't really know what she's talking about. My head is spinning. What has happened to my sulky, silent, grumpy sister? She's suddenly become an expert in all of this and she won't stop talking.

"And when I was chatting to Vicky, she told me about the different ways artists play with gender and challenge all these social norms. It's really interesting, Izzy. You should look at some of the stuff she's sent me. It's like nothing you've seen before."

This is typical Megan. She's always so sure about everything. She knows exactly what she thinks and you can't argue with her. Even if she changes her mind about something, she acts as though she's always thought this way and you're the one who's got it wrong. Like when she was in seventh grade and went overnight from loving pot roast dinners to being a total vegetarian. Then if you asked her if she missed meat, she looked at you like you were mad.

"Do you think that's how people in my class know?" I ask, as we walk down the steps into the underpass. "Because you've been telling people?"

"I don't know. I don't think so. I can't really imagine many high schoolers spending much time hanging out with seventh-graders—except for me, unfortunately," says Megan. "But so what if they do know? I bet there are plenty of people with things they want to keep hidden about their families. I bet there are other people at school who know someone who's trans, or who are trans themselves. I mean, there must be."

"Mmm," I say, thinking about Sam and his secret.

"Anyone gives you trouble—it's their problem, not yours. Here, let me show you something." Megan gets her phone out of her pocket and starts scrolling through before she shows me an image. There's black capital lettering on a bright red background. The lettering says: *Some people are trans. Get over it.*

"There are other ones, too. *Some people are gay. Get over it. Some people are bi. Get over it.* Stuff like that. It means if people in your year are giving you grief, *they* are the ones who need to get over it. Not you."

I like it. It looks so simple written down in block letters. Even if it isn't that simple in real life. I imagine myself saying, "Get over it," to Lucas or Mia, Charlie or Olivia. But I can't. I'm too shy. I *can* imagine Grace doing it, not caring about whether she upsets people. All *I* want is for people to like me, or to leave me alone.

"They should do other ones," I say.

"How do you mean?"

"Like, *Some people are shy. Get over it.* Or . . ." I glance over at Megan. "*Some people are grumpy. Get over it.*"

"Hmm," she says. "I don't know who you're talking about. What about, *Some sisters are annoying. Get over it?*"

"Only some sisters," I say. "And only sometimes."

We separate at the school gates, Megan walking over to the art room to hand in some work, and me dashing up the main steps, almost falling over Mr. Thomas, who's coming the other way carrying a huge stack of colored paper.

"I was hoping to bump into you today, Isabel," he says. "Although maybe not quite so literally. Are you feeling better? We missed you yesterday."

"Yes, much better, Mr. Thomas."

"Well, don't worry, you haven't missed all the fun."

My mind is totally blank. "What fun?"

He points to the pile of programs in his arms. "Folding these. They were late getting copied, so we couldn't get them ready yesterday after all. So if you've got time this lunchtime, it's all hands on deck. . . ."

"Oh, yes, of course, I'll try," I murmur.

I feel my newfound confidence draining away as I get closer to the classroom door. Get over it? Yeah, right. Megan and I must have walked really fast, because I'm not too late after all. The seats where Grace and I normally sit, by the window in the middle on the left, are still empty, so I sit down and start getting my books out. I'm careful not to look at anyone, but when Sheetal smiles at me and waves from the other side of the classroom, I smile shyly back.

Charlotte leans over from the desk behind, and asks me a question about homework, just like nothing's changed and I feel like perhaps it's going to be okay. I turn around to her and start explaining what I put in the essay. After a few seconds her eyes shift away, and she looks over my shoulder. Grace's come in.

She walks straight past me without even looking, to the empty place next to Olivia.

"Okay if I sit here?" she asks.

"Yeah, sure," says Olivia, looking a bit surprised. "Aren't you sitting with Izzy, though?"

"No," says Grace airily. "I don't think so. Not today. I don't have to always do the same thing, or always hang out with the same people, do I?"

In the end, no one sits next to me. I can hear Olivia and Grace at the back of the classroom, whispering and giggling, and tears prick at my eyes. *Get over it, get over it, get over it.*

As Miss Abbott drones on about river basins, I think about what I'm going to say to Grace. I can't leave things like this. I try out the lines in my head, searching for the right words, the right intonation, that will make it all okay. She can't really mean those things she said. Just like I didn't really mean what I said to her.

I've just got it all straight and on the tip of my tongue when the bell goes, and the classroom explodes with noise and bustle.

I get as far as, "Grace, I . . ." as she walks past my desk. But my throat's dry and my voice comes out faint and squeaky. She looks at me, and opens her mouth to say something, and then Olivia grabs her arm and says, "Come on, Grace, let's go," and all of a sudden she's walking away, with only a quick glance back at me. I'm left standing there, mouth open, words wasted.

At recess, I don't know what to do. I think about approaching Grace again, but she's surrounded by people. I don't want to make a fool of myself in front of Olivia and the others. I don't want people feeling sorry for me. Poor little Izzy.

It feels like it did when I was in grammar school, before I really had friends, before I knew Grace. Then recess used to feel like it stretched on and on for hours—with everyone else in their little groups, talking or skipping or playing together. Me on the edge.

There were things I used to do then to make recess go faster. I'd walk around the edge of the playground, imagining I had somewhere important to go, counting my steps or reciting the words to my favorite songs in my head.

The grounds are much bigger at St. Mary's than they were at Woodside, so it takes me almost the whole of recess to get around them. But I don't succeed in convincing myself, let alone anyone who might be watching.

The other thing I used to do, especially when it was winter, was to go to the bathroom and then stay in there as long as I could. No one usually noticed I was gone, and it was a quiet place to sit and think.

It's biology next, so I make my way to the girls' toilets outside the science room and settle into the end cubicle for a bit of peace in the last few minutes of recess.

It's not especially peaceful, with the sound of doors banging and toilets flushing echoing off the tiled walls. It's a bit dark and smelly—although probably not as bad as the boys'—but at least no one knows I'm here. I'm just about to come out when I hear voices I recognize. I freeze.

"Oh my god, look at my hair. It's frizzing everywhere. I look like I've had an electric shock." It's Charlotte.

"Here, you can use my comb," says Olivia's voice, and I hear her rummaging through her bag. "So what do you think's happened with Izzy and Grace?" she continues.

"Don't know, it's really weird," says Charlotte. "Hasn't she said anything to you?"

"What, Grace?"

"Of course Grace. Who else have you been with all morning?"

"No, nothing. Hey, don't put it in your bag, it's my comb."

"Sorry, here you go."

"Anyway, you can't make Grace talk about something she doesn't want to talk about, like with this thing with Izzy's dad. Obviously Grace knew all about it, and never said anything."

I'm holding my breath as I listen, trying not to make a

sound. I don't want to hear anymore, but I can't stop myself straining to listen. Anyway, what else can I do? I can't come bursting out now without looking like I was deliberately spying on them.

"That's weird, too. I can't imagine what it'd be like if *my* dad decided to have—" she lowers her voice into a whisper "—a sex change. I'd die of shame. Poor Izzy. It's like something out of a magazine."

So much for what Grace said, that everyone would have forgotten about it after a day. Some chance. I put my hand to my face—it's gone hot with embarrassment. I'm glad no one can see me in here.

"Your mom'd go mad," replies Olivia firmly. "She'd never let him out of the house again!" They both laugh and the door slams behind them.

It's suddenly quiet. And I feel even more alone than I did before.

Chapter Nineteen

I'm deliberately late into the cafeteria. I'm ravenous. If I skip lunch I'll feel even worse, so I know I have to eat something.

Grace is sitting wedged between Olivia and Charlotte, picking at chips. I choose a spot at the end of a table of sixth-graders, who are talking so excitedly about who's going to get picked for the next kickball match that they don't even notice me.

After a couple of minutes, Charlotte walks over. "Hey, Izzy, there's space with us if you want to come over," she says, smiling kindly. Is she really being friendly, or is it just because she's feeling sorry for me? I remember what she said to Olivia, when she didn't know I was there. *Poor Izzy.*

I smile as confidently as I can, and say, "No, thanks,

that's really nice, Charlotte, but I'm nearly finished, honestly."

"Well . . ." she says, lingering by my place, glancing at my piled-high plate of pasta. "Well, if you're sure. . . . You can always come over if you change your mind."

"Thanks, I will." But I won't. I'd rather be by myself than have people taking pity on me. At least, that's what I think for the next five minutes.

But then I'm stuck. I'm too embarrassed to go over— why should Charlotte bother to be nice to me again now?—though I don't fancy spending the whole of lunchtime hiding in the girls' bathroom or wandering by myself in the cold.

I could go and find Megan, but she'll be over in the high school wing. Anyway, we don't tend to talk to each other when we're at school. However friendly she was this morning, I'm not sure she'd fancy her little sister crowding in on her and her friends.

Then I remember Mr. Thomas. Of course. I can head over to the drama studio and fold programs. It'll be warm, and no one will dare say anything, because Mr. Thomas will be there. I scarf down my bolognese, check to see that Grace and the others are still busy with their lunch, and then make my way to the studio.

"Isabel!" says Mr. Thomas, jumping up and beaming at me as I come through the door. "You star! You've saved me. I thought my fingers were going to fall off. Lots of people said they'd come yesterday, but when it got postponed, no one remembered to come back today. Except you." He pauses. "You *are* here to fold programs, aren't you?"

There are stacks of colored paper on a table at the far corner of the room with plastic chairs set around it. Mr. Thomas sits back down on a chair, cradling a chipped "Best Teacher Ever" mug in his hands. He's one of those people who always looks like they are moving, even when they are sitting still.

"Yes, here I am," I say. "Just tell me what I need to do."

"Okay so, take a seat. The yellow ones are Thursday, the green ones are Friday, and the red ones are Saturday, do you see?" he says, indicating each pile. "But that doesn't matter, because they all fold the same. I've made a start, though there's a lot more still to go."

It's the first time I've seen the programs close up. A shiver goes right down my back: There's my name listed next to Sarah Brown and Grace's right underneath, in black ink, copied hundreds of times.

"Exciting, isn't it?" says Mr. Thomas. "And maybe a little bit scary?"

I nod. "It means it's really going to happen."

"You bet it is. You know, all the best performers get nervous before they go onstage. It's natural."

I raise my eyebrows. I'm not sure I believe him. That's the sort of trying-to-make-you-feel-better thing that people say whether it's true or not.

"It's true," he insists. "I mean, think about the singer Adele. I heard that she gets really anxious before performing. Once it got so bad that she projectile vomited on someone before a show just because of her nerves."

I make a face. "Yuck."

"Sorry, you probably didn't need to know that. But my point is, it's okay to be nervous. It means that you care."

It's a bit awkward at first, just me and Mr. Thomas. But he doesn't seem to mind that it looks like no one else is coming, and secretly I'm quite glad.

I haven't spent this much time just me and a teacher before. But I relax as he chats on—he seems to know tons of showbiz gossip—and gradually the pile of folded programs between us grows higher. The rhythm of lining up and folding and stacking is soothing. I wish I could do this all day.

I wonder about Mr. Thomas. He doesn't have kids, or if he does, he never talks about them. He doesn't seem old enough anyway. He doesn't wear a wedding ring—but then lots of people don't. What's he like when he's not being a teacher? Is there a Mrs. Thomas—or does he sit at home by himself reading celebrity magazines and marking our homework?

He's not from Littlehaven, I know that much. Although I don't know why anyone would choose to come and live here. He's got a Scottish accent and teases us sometimes about how all the best poetry and all the best inventions come from Scotland, not from England.

"Why did you move to Littlehaven?" I ask out loud, and then wonder quickly if that's too risky a question. Too late now. Anyway, Grace would have no worries about asking something that personal.

Mr. Thomas sighs, looking serious. "The old story, Isabel. Love. I met someone from here. I came to live here. It didn't work out. They left. And I stayed. Although that's not quite the end of the story." He straightens another pile of programs by tapping them down loudly on the table. Then he smiles at me. "Anyway, why wouldn't I stay? I get to run the best drama department in the county, put on all my favorite shows, and teach some fantastic students...." He looks straight at me and I blush.

"Now I've answered your question, would you like to

know one of my guilty secrets?" Before I can answer, he opens his briefcase and, with a dramatic flourish, pulls out a shiny, black-and-blue packet. "Oreos," he says gleefully. "Can't get enough of them. Made in the U.S. for over a hundred years, millions sold every day—a fair few of them to me." He waves the packet at me. "Would you like one?"

I take a cookie, of course, and eat it carefully to avoid getting crumbs on the programs.

After a little while of chewing and folding without either of us talking, Mr. Thomas says, "Are you all right, Isabel? How is life treating you at the moment?"

I carry on folding, silently and steadily. Looking down at the programs. I wonder if Mr. Thomas knows about my dad and Grace and Sam and Lucas and everything, if people are talking about me behind my back and everything about my life is public knowledge. My mouth's still full of sweet, sticky cookie. I'm glad because it means I don't have to answer.

"You don't have to talk about anything you don't want to," he carries on quietly. "But if you do want to talk to me, then, well, I'm here. My job isn't just nagging you to hand in your homework or boring you with ancient poetry, you know, my job's to listen."

Suddenly, the door of the studio bangs open, letting in the cold air.

"Mr. Thomas, I totally forgot all about the programs. I hope it's not too late to lend a hand," says Mia breathlessly. "I've reminded some of the others as well, they're just on their way over." She looks over at me, and a scowl flashes across her face. She quickly pastes her smile back on, but not quickly enough, I still see her real expression. "Oh, Izzy, hello, you're already here."

"Actually, Mia, Isabel and I have been making fine progress. We're almost there. But there are a few more to do, so it's great to have some extra hands on deck. Go on, take a seat."

Mia picks a chair as far away from me as possible and stretches out her long legs under the table.

I check my watch and there's only ten minutes of lunch hour left. I pick up my bag. I'm sure I can keep a low profile somewhere else till the bell sounds.

"Well, it looks like you'll get it all finished without me now. I'd better go and get my books ready. I'll see you later," I say, heading quickly toward the door.

"Thanks for your hard work," says Mr. Thomas with a smile. "And don't forget what I said, will you?"

Chapter Twenty

This must have been the longest week in the history of the world. I can't believe that only a week ago, no one knew about Dee, and Grace and I were still best friends. And yesterday must have been the longest day of the longest week, going even slower than a normal Friday. Grace and I carried on avoiding each other. No one said anything horrible to my face, but no one went out of their way to be nice to me either.

"What's up with you?" says Mom, as I mooch around the kitchen on Saturday morning, picking at food left on the side and flicking through the free newspapers. "Wherever I go this morning, you're under my feet. And you look pale. Are you still a bit under the weather?"

"I don't think so," I say reluctantly. I quite enjoyed

Mom looking after me when I was out of school on Tuesday. "I feel all right now."

"So what are you up to today? Is Grace coming over?" It's a perfectly normal question for a Saturday morning, but it makes me wonder what Mom has noticed over the last few days.

I shake my head.

"It's just I haven't seen her much this week." She pauses thoughtfully. "Is everything all right with you two?"

"Yes, well, no. Sort of…" I momble.

Mom stops drying up and turns to look at me. Her voice softens. "Whatever it is, it'll sort itself out, I promise," she says, drying her hands on a dish towel before putting her arm briefly round my shoulders in a kind of half hug. So brief that you could almost miss it.

She moves away to stack the dishes in the cupboard. "Look, why don't you come into town with me? I've got to take Jamie to a birthday party—" she rolls her eyes "—not exactly my favorite thing, but I can drop you off first. It'd give you something to do instead of moping round here, making a mess."

"Mom, I don't know. Perhaps I'll just go back to bed, or read a book or something. I don't know if I can be bothered to go into town."

167

"Come on, you can do a bit of window-shopping. . . ."

"I hate window-shopping."

Mom smiles. "Yeah, okay, so do I. But I still think it would do you good to get out. I'm offering you a ride, remember? That doesn't happen very often. You could go to the library, get out some books to help with your homework. . . . You're probably a bit too big for the birthday play, but we could try and sneak you in. . . ."

"Ha ha, very funny."

But what else am I going to do? It's better than just staying at home feeling miserable; I might as well go with Mom.

An hour later, she drops me off on Main Street, with strict instructions to meet her back there in an hour and a half. Jamie's full of excitement about his party, and chats all the way about how he's going to go on the biggest slide and who he's going to bury in the ball pool. I just sit in silence and dream, soothed by the movement of the car. Perhaps I could go to sleep now and wake up to find none of this has happened, just like they do in films.

I'm still in a dream when I'm standing outside a bodega, looking at the chocolate. I'd normally get a Kit Kat, and then Grace and I would split it half each. But now it's just me, I'm not even sure what I want. I've probably been standing there for a few minutes when I hear a voice behind me.

"Hello, Isabel." I snap out of my dream and turn round to face Grace's mom. Her hands are full of bulging shopping bags. "How are you, my love?" she says with a huge smile, resting her bags down on the floor. I look around the shop quickly, panicking, to see if Grace's there, too, but there's only a kid about Jamie's age looking at the magazines with his mom.

Grace's mom works out what I'm doing. I guess it's pretty obvious. "No, Grace's at home. Getting on with some homework, so she says. What about you? Are you here with your mom?"

I shake my head. "No, Mom's taken Jamie to a party. She's going to pick me up in a bit."

Grace's mom looks at me long and hard, as if she's trying to work out a puzzle in her head. "You don't need to get yourself any chocolate here," she says finally. "I've finished my shopping, and you've got a bit of time. Come on, let's go and get ourselves something proper to eat. Take a couple of these bags, would you, my love? I know just the place."

Before I know it, I'm following her down the street. She's not quite as chatty as Grace, but I'm still relieved that I don't have to do too much to contribute to the conversation. Just a few "uh-huh"s and "really?"s seem to do the job.

We turn off for the Corner Café. It's an odd name for a café that isn't actually on a corner. Instead it's sandwiched between a pub and a secondhand shop down one of the side streets. But once you're inside, the name makes sense. Somehow, they've created a space full of little private corners, with padded booths and comfy chairs. The lights are low and the walls are lined with bookshelves and framed quotes. Tables aren't squashed up next to each other, and there's no risk of overhearing someone else's conversation. Much to my relief.

We sit down in one of the booths, barricaded in by bags. Grace's mom kicks off her shoes and orders us both chocolate cake. She gets a large steaming cup of coffee and I get a banana milkshake with whipped cream.

"I love coming here," she says. "It's a real treat. When I want a bit of cake—that I haven't made myself, that is. I know I won't be disappointed."

When our drinks come with the bill, I fumble awkwardly for my purse. Grace's mom quickly puts her hand on my arm. "My treat," she says firmly. "To say thank you for being such a good friend to my Grace."

I feel awful. It's not like Grace and I have been the best

of friends this week. I don't know if we will ever be again.

"I mean it," she continues. "You're such a good influence on her. You calm her down, you know, she's always full of excitement, getting carried away about everything. She needs a friend with a cooler, calmer head on her shoulders.

"And you need her as well, I think, don't you? That's why God made us all different, to bear each other's burdens."

Grace's mom talks about God like he's someone who just lives down the street, casually popping his name into conversation, passing on the news of what he's been up to and what he thinks about things. Not like Mom and Dad—they're not religious at all. They didn't even have us christened when we were babies.

I don't know what I think, only that any god who says Dee's an abomination is not someone I want anything to do with. Surely someone as warm and kind as Grace's mom wouldn't believe in that sort of god either. But then what about what Grace said? I push the question away, but it keeps coming back.

I nod and try to swallow a mouthful of chocolate cake. It is amazing, all gooey and crumbly, but my mouth's gone dry.

Grace's mom is still going. "I'm glad I ran into you today

actually. It's none of my business, I suppose, but things aren't quite right with you and Grace at the moment, are they?" She takes a large sip from her coffee and looks up at me.

"I don't need to know what it's about," she says, dabbing the milky coffee from around her mouth with her napkin. "Unless you want to tell me. But whatever it is, it will blow over, I'm sure. I know what Grace is like. Everything's a big drama, and then she calms down, and wonders what on earth she got so worked up about. She'll come around. Anyway, how are you enjoying your milkshake? You know they put ice cream in it as well?"

"It's delicious, thank you," I say. And it is, I've almost reached the bottom of the glass, there's just the last mouthful still to savor.

"And how are you, my love? And the rest of the family? Has that sweet little brother of yours started school yet?"

"Yeah, Jamie's in kindergarten now," I say. "He's loving school, thinks his teacher's the best thing ever. He's always coming home with stars and stickers. And Megan started her junior year."

"My goodness, sounds like your mom must have her hands full, what with the three of you all at such different stages."

"I guess so." I shrug. "Mom's got lots of work, too, at the moment, which is good, I suppose, but she's always really busy."

"And your dad?"

"Oh, Dad, well . . ." I start, but tail off, not sure what to say. Then it dawns on me, she already knows.

"Sorry, Isabel," she says, spreading out her hands. "Littlehaven's a small town."

"Yeah, I know." I even manage to smile. Somehow Grace's mom always makes me feel comfortable, like I can say anything to her. "I'm learning there are no secrets here."

There's a silence, while we both scrape the last crumbs from our plates.

"It must be—" I can see Grace's mom searching for the right word "—different . . . with your dad now."

"Yes, I suppose it is. But in lots of ways everything's kind of the same, even though it's all changing, too. Oh, I don't know, most of the time it's not Dad that I worry about, it's everybody else: what they think, what they say, what they don't say, what I think they're going to say."

She smiles. "Sounds complicated."

I feel like I've already said too much. I couldn't bear it if she said anything bad about Dee now. But I screw up my courage. I've got this far, I can keep going.

"Can I ask you something?"

"Of course, my love. Ask away."

It comes out all in a rush. It's the only way I can get the words out without crying. "Do-you-think-my-dad's-an-abomination?"

She's so surprised that she chokes on her coffee and starts coughing violently. I offer to get her a glass of water, but she just flaps her hands around and shakes her head.

When things have calmed down, she says, "Oh, my life. Of course not, why on earth would you think that?"

"Well, Grace said, I mean, she said that Pastor Johnson said...."

"Oh, that girl," interrupts Grace's mom in exasperation. "She never pays any attention in church—and then comes out with the most ridiculous, thoughtless things. I'm so sorry."

"But what about the Bible? Doesn't it say that?" I desperately hope that Grace has somehow got it mixed-up.

"The Bible says lots of things, my love. It was written a long time ago and times have changed since then. But do you know one thing it says that's never going to change?"

I shake my head.

"'Love your neighbor,'" she says firmly. "'Don't judge

other people.' Simple as that."

"Love your neighbor." Nice idea, but really? That's it?

Grace's mom sighs. "Let me tell you about something that happened to me. Is that all right? It's only fair. You never met Grace's dad," she continues thoughtfully. "He's been gone such a long time now. I don't know if even Grace remembers much about him. He was such a charming man. So good-looking. I thought I had such a catch."

It's embarrassing, hearing someone's mom talking like this. I shift in my seat.

She shakes her head. She's not even looking at me anymore. "But he left. Grace was only a tiny thing. He left for someone else, and that was that. Gone. I was in pieces.

"And my friends in the church were there. They helped me to lift my head again, to not blame myself for everything." She stops and looks down, slowly smoothing her napkin out on the table.

"Not everyone was like that, though. It was just little things, but I could sense something changed after Marcus left. I stopped being asked to help out with certain things. Fewer people would ask me over. I could feel some of the women staring at me suspiciously when I even just talked to their husbands. No one said anything, not to me, but I knew what they were thinking—I must have done something wrong, or Marcus would have stayed with me."

"That's so unfair," I say.

"I know, my love, I know. But things aren't always fair, are they?" I nod firmly. She's right. Things aren't fair. What's fair about people laughing at me just because of something my dad's done? Something which shouldn't matter to anyone else anyway?

"But why didn't you leave, if people were so horrible to you?"

I remember the singing and the smiling and how everyone seemed so friendly. It didn't seem like the sort of place where people gossiped and made other people feel bad. Perhaps none of the things I think I know and none of the people I think I can trust can be relied on anymore.

"Because, well, because whatever happens, the people at church are still my family. And I'm still there to worship God, just as much as anyone else. Even if sometimes I lay awake wondering if God was punishing me, I knew it wasn't my fault that Marcus left. And I knew my God wasn't in the business of handing out punishments. There's enough trouble in this world already. That's why I think it's no one's business to pass judgement on someone else, whoever they are. You hear me, Isabel, don't you?"

I nod.

"Good. I'd better be getting on home," she says, standing up. "And you need to get back to meet your mom. It's been lovely seeing you, Isabel. You know you are welcome at our house anytime. Now make sure you send my good wishes to your parents, won't you?"

"Thanks, Mrs. Okafor," I say. And I mean it. I didn't even say anything much, but for the first time in days, I feel light again, not like I'm about to burst into tears any moment. There's still Dee and Grace and even Sam Kenner to worry about, but the weight in my stomach doesn't feel so heavy anymore.

Chapter Twenty-One

It's December. Nearly the end of year and less than a week till the first night of the show. When we began rehearsals in September, it seemed like we'd have forever to get it right. But now time's running out. Mr. Thomas has put in an extra rehearsal after school today, the first one where no scripts are allowed. Even though it means staying late on a Friday, no one's complained. We all know we need the extra practice.

"What are you muttering?" asks Megan over breakfast.

"I'm just going over my lines," I say, walking my fingers across the highlighted words. "No scripts today."

"Wow, scary stuff." She smiles.

This new Megan, the one who actually speaks to me, and even smiles, appears to still be around. It gives me the confidence to ask, "Will you test me? It'll only take a minute. We can do it as we walk in." I point at the crumpled pages. "Look, my lines are the ones in yellow."

I've given up expecting Grace to come for me now. It's been over a week since she last called but, strangely, I'm quite enjoying walking in with Megan. Mom must know what's going on, but she hasn't asked anything about where Grace is since Saturday.

That's what I've noticed over the last few weeks: We *don't* say anything. When something's wrong or difficult or awkward, we barely talk about it. Only if there's no other option. Vicky does. Grace's mom does. Even Mr. Thomas tries to. But not us.

Are all families like this? Always skating carefully round the difficult stuff? Mom and Dee say they're always happy to talk, but I don't think they are, not really. I don't even think they'd have said anything about the transition if they thought they could get away without us seeing, if they thought we wouldn't notice that Dad was becoming a woman.

I like it this way, I think, not having to always think and talk and rake over how I'm feeling. At least then we don't fall down any cracks into icy waters. But sometimes silence isn't enough.

We definitely haven't talked about the thing that's worrying me most right now: Dee coming to the show. They haven't mentioned it and I can't find the words. Dee and Mom seem so much more chilled than they've been for ages, so I don't want to spoil things. I know they're excited about coming, and I really want them to be there. But . . .

Even if everyone already knows, it's different from them seeing her, from her actually coming into school, where everyone—my friends, the teachers, other people's parents—will be laughing or whispering or trying not to look.

"Sorry, Izzy, I can't help you with your lines, I need to get into the art room early," Megan says, interrupting my thoughts. "I'm entering the art prize and there's not long to go. It's not just your show that's happening at the end of term, you know?"

The art prize is a Big Thing. If Megan hadn't been so sulky and cross and silent, and if I'd been less caught up in *Guys and Dolls*, I'd have worked out before now that she'd be entering. Especially because she fancies herself as this great artist.

The prize is named after some famous artist who once visited the school. Not someone actually from Littlehaven, obviously, this place is much too boring for that. But someone who, bizarrely, came here and liked it enough to leave some money in their will for an annual art prize. Personally, I could think of much better things to spend my money on. Even after I was dead.

It means that at the end of every Christmas break, all the high school students get to work on their masterpieces. The entries are displayed on the walls and around the edges of the school halls. They're all unveiled at once, so one morning you come in and the halls are no longer shabby and dull like usual. They're transformed with huge paintings and crazy sculptures, suddenly full of color.

"So, what are you painting?"

"Ah, that's for me to know . . ." she says, tapping the side of her nose and using one of Mom's favourite phrases.

". . . And me to find out. Yeah, yeah, I know. But why the big secret?"

"Cos it's a surprise, nosy. That makes it more fun. Anyway, who says I'm *painting* anything? I'm not really sure it's going to work yet. And I have to go. Now."

I trudge into school by myself, that familiar feeling of dread settling back into my stomach as I get nearer to the gates. I try to take my mind off it by going over my lines in my head, but I keep getting stuck at the bit when Sarah and Sky first meet. I can't help imagining looking out into the audience as I say my lines and seeing Dee.

When it's time for rehearsal, Sam falls into step with me as I hurry down the corridor to the drama studio. Everyone else is pouring out of their classrooms and heading in the opposite direction. It's so loud and there's so much jostling that I don't notice he's there until a voice close to my ear says hello.

It makes me jump. And that makes me blush. We haven't talked properly, not about anything that really matters, since he turned up on our doorstep a week ago.

"Sorry to startle you. I must stop doing that." He smiles. "Know your lines?"

"Kind of. I think so anyway. You?"

"Most of them. I'll be okay—as long as you help me out if I get stuck. And promise not to step on my feet."

"Oh, sorry, I really, that was a . . ." I stutter.

"Just joking, Izzy." He raises his eyebrows, and I relax. "I'm sure I put my feet in the wrong place, that's all. Anyway, today's the moment of truth. Mr. Thomas wouldn't do it if he didn't think we were ready."

"Hmm, maybe," I say. "Or maybe he thinks we'll never be ready, but it's still got to happen sometime. Your parents coming?"

"Yeah, first night. They've got their tickets already. They're dragging my brother along, too. He's ten, and thinks that singing and dancing are really lame. He wasn't even impressed when I told him that I'm going to be this smooth-talking gangster."

"My parents are bringing my little brother, too," I say. "He's really excited. He hasn't got a clue what it's about, but he's thrilled about coming into 'big school' with me and Megan. It's kind of cute. It ends way past his bedtime, so he'll probably fall asleep halfway through."

Sam smiles. "Just as long as the rest of the audience don't do that, we'll be okay."

"Oh my god, what if they do? What if they all start snoring?" I giggle, imagining all the hall chairs slumped full of sleeping parents, like the kingdom in *Sleeping Beauty*, while we all carry on to a chorus of snores.

"And your dad's coming . . . ?" Sam says, more softly. He tails off, but I know just what he was going to ask.

"Yeah," I say, lowering my voice to match his, although the corridors have emptied out and there's no one nearby. "It'll be the first time she's been into school, though, since, you know . . ." I sigh. "It's just that there'll be so many people at the show."

Sam looks at me closely. "You'd rather she wasn't coming?" he asks gently, not seeming fazed at all by saying "she."

"No, it's not that." I shake my head. "Of course I want her there. It's just that I wish things were normal again— but they're not. Anyway, Megan and me, we're calling Dad 'Dee' now, and trying to remember to say 'she' not 'he' . . . I try, but I keep forgetting."

"That must be weird to get used to."

"It's just hard to remember, that's all. What about you and your dad?"

"Well, I've never known anything else. He's always just been Dad. I hardly even think about it." He pauses. "Except in the last few days. Since talking to you, I've been thinking about it a lot."

Before he can say anymore, we stop short outside the drama-studio door. The smoothness of the conversation has gone, and the awkwardness is back again.

"Well," I say, "here we go."

Chapter Twenty-Two

Sam pushes open the door. We're a little late, but Mr. Thomas isn't there yet, just clusters of cast members poring over their scripts or testing each other on their lines. Two boys working on the lighting are hunched over a laptop in the corner arguing about spotlights.

Grace's surrounded by people: Charlotte, Olivia, Sheetal, a few other girls. She carries on talking and laughing, while shooting me and Sam a look as we come in together. I can't describe it. She doesn't look angry or jealous. Just kind of tired and lost. Very un-Grace, in fact.

"Hey, Sam, come and look at this," someone calls, and Sam moves off with a quick nod to join a huddle of boys.

I find a spot to perch on a table at the other end of the room and unfold the crumpled pages of my script. The lines are swimming before my eyes. I look up, and my heart sinks as I see Mia coming over.

"Hello, Izzy," she says in her sickly sweet voice. I nod and look back to my script, hoping she'll go away, but she still sits down next to me.

"All by yourself again today?" she asks, talking a little bit too loud, like she wants everyone else to hear. "Poor Izzy. Been dumped by your girlfriend, have you?"

I stop pretending to read, and just stare at her.

"What, so surprised?" she carries on in a fake, shocked voice. The room goes quiet. "Everyone knows you fancy her, Izzy, that you're gay. After all, it's obvious . . . that sort of thing runs in families, doesn't it? That's why we've all been keeping our distance. Got to be careful after all."

Before I can say or do anything, there's a rush from the other side of the room. There's Grace, standing right over Mia, looking as fierce as I've ever seen her.

"Mia Harrison, you just shut your fat mouth before any more garbage comes out," she shouts. "And keep your nose out of other people's business. No one wants to know what you think. Izzy's not gay and she's not my girlfriend. But if she was, I'd be really proud. She's kind and thoughtful and funny, which means she's *nothing* like you. Come on, Izzy."

Then she grabs me by the arm, and marches me out of the studio. The last thing I see, before the door bangs loudly behind us, is Mia's face. All the color's drained out of it, and she looks like she's just been slapped.

Grace crouches down with her back against the wall, eyes shut, breathing deeply.

It's been so long since we last spoke.

"Did you mean all of that?" I ask cautiously.

Grace opens her eyes and looks up.

"Yeah," she says. "Every word. Although I wouldn't *really* want to be your girlfriend." She smiles up at me. "Not unless you were as hot as Sam Kenner."

I tense up, but it seems that Grace isn't going to have a go at me about Sam today.

"Ohhh," she groans. "I shouldn't have said all those things about Mia, should I? Did I really tell her to shut her fat mouth?"

I nod. "You were amazing," I say. "But I'm not sure she'll ever speak to you, or me, again."

"Well, that suits me fine."

"It was like you were Miss Adelaide, telling off Nathan," I say admiringly. "It was really dramatic." I know that when she calms down, Grace's going to enjoy retelling and reliving this scene for weeks to come.

I wonder what's going to happen now. Does Grace sticking up for me mean we're friends again? Or is it just pity? Or the fact she hates Mia even more than she hates me?

"We'd better go back in. Mr. Thomas will be here in a minute," says Grace, pushing herself up to standing and smoothing out her skirt.

I hesitate. She looks back.

"Come on then," she calls over her shoulder and, as usual, I follow.

Chapter Twenty-Three

Dress rehearsal day. It's come pretty quickly. I can hardly believe that tomorrow's the first night and we'll be performing in front of a real audience.

Half of me can't stop thinking of all the things that could go wrong, and all the people that will be watching when they do. And the other half is bursting with excitement, itching to be up onstage, and already feeling sad about how soon it will be over.

Unfortunately, either way, it's like there's a troupe of elephants tap-dancing in my stomach.

I can't help wondering how Grace is feeling. She always looks so full of confidence on the outside, but I know for sure she'll be nervous inside. I've been imagining the dress rehearsal ever since we first heard we'd got the main parts.

The two of us practicing our lines together, checking our makeup, calming each other's nerves, chatting all the way home about what went right and what went wrong. But I guess that's not how it's going to be. It was amazing how she stuck up for me against Mia on Friday. I hoped that after the weekend, things would go back to normal again but this week we've barely spoken, let alone sat together or walked to and from school. Nothing seems to have changed, so I suppose she just felt sorry for me.

Poor little Izzy.

Everyone at home is caught up in the excitement of the show. I've heard Dee whistling the tunes around the house, and Mom's not said a word about homework this week. Jamie keeps asking me over and over again, *Is it today? Is it today?*

Everyone except Megan. She's shut up in her room or in the high school wing, working all the time on her mysterious composition. It's still a big secret—all she says is that it's a mixed-media installation piece, and that doesn't help at all.

The kitchen's full. Megan's hunched over her phone. Jamie's shoveling cereal down his throat, splattering milk everywhere. Mom's bustling around, turning over piles of paper looking for the car keys.

Dee's still here for once—she's going straight to see someone's house before going into the office. She's sitting at the table, engrossed in the paper, tutting and sighing as she reads.

"What's the big news?" I ask.

"Huh?" she replies, without looking up.

"In the paper. What's so interesting?"

"Oh, nothing." She quickly folds the paper over, and tucks it away in her bag, looking like a naughty child caught doing something they shouldn't, and changes the subject. "So, Izzy, it's the big day, isn't it? Well, the day before the big day, I should say. How are you feeling? All ready?"

I say, "Well, there are still a few hard parts. . . ."

Dee laughs. "You know what they say, the worse the dress rehearsal, the better the first night. So, for your sake, I hope there *are* still a few hard bits, so that tomorrow it runs like clockwork. We can't wait to see it, can we, Kath?"

"Mmm," says Mom absentmindedly, turning out her bag on the kitchen table and spreading out the contents.

"Remember when we did *Singing in the Rain* in middle school?" Dee continues. "The dress rehearsal was a total nightmare—I forgot half my lines, your mom had to keep helping me out, and the set wasn't even finished. We had to step over paint pots and brushes. Some kid—what was his name? All gangly arms and legs, played Cosmo—tripped over and got his costume covered in paint."

"James Findhorn," says Mom. "How come I can remember that useless information from twenty years ago, but not where I put the car keys yesterday? We should have a place for these things," she adds accusingly.

"Why didn't you say?" says Dee, fishing them out of her bag and sliding them across the table.

The edge of the newspaper is still sticking out of the bag. It's not a paper we usually get, so Dee must have gone out early especially to buy it.

I tilt my head sideways to read the headline. All I can see is:

<u>**GRAM**</u>

<u>**KID**</u>

<u>**INT**</u>

in huge, black, underlined letters.

It's like a puzzle, trying to work out the hidden letters. My mind latches onto it as a distraction from trying to remember my lines.

"Grammar . . . kidney . . . international?" I murmur to myself. "Grammar . . . kids . . . international?"

I pull the paper out of the bag and smooth it out on the

table to read the headline in full. Megan puts her phone away and cranes over to look at it, too:

GRAMMAR SCHOOL
KIDS FORCED
INTO SEX CHANGE

"Oh," I say.

Everyone goes quiet, apart from the sound of Jamie eating with his mouth open. No one even tells him off.

"You might as well read the article," says Dee finally. "Just make sure you don't believe a word of it. There was a report released yesterday. About people who are transgender and the kind of support they need. At school, at work, from the DOH, that kind of thing. And somehow *that* has become a story like *this*." She gestures to the paper and screws up her face in disgust.

"So, it's not true?" I ask.

"No, Izzy, it's not true," says Dee. "It's twisted and mean and not true."

"That's terrible!" Megan says, as I skim the article. "Printing lies that thousands of people will read over breakfast and not know any better."

"More like hundreds of thousands," says Dee glumly.

"Hundreds of millions of billions of thousands," says Jamie, finding a way to get into the conversation.

"Just because it's in the papers, or on the internet, for that matter, doesn't make it true. You're both clever girls, you know that."

"I'm clever, too," pipes up Jamie. "Aren't I, Izzy?"

"But still," I persist, "someone should say something, right? They should print what this report's really about. The other side of the story."

"What's the point? It's already out there. No one's even questioning if it's true or not," sighs Dee, as she pulls herself up out of her chair. It's strange, she's been so much happier and more relaxed in the last few weeks that I'd almost forgotten how gloomy she could sometimes be. Especially before, when she was just "Dad." I guess it's like Mom said, now she doesn't have to keep a secret anymore, it's like she can be fully here, with us, not lost in her own thoughts and worries, the way Dad could sometimes be before. I would never have expected it to be this way, but there are some good things about all of these changes.

"I don't see why you're giving up," I say loudly, banging my mug down on the kitchen table. "It's just not fair, that's what I think, and I know you do too. It shouldn't be allowed."

Mom and Megan look up in surprise. I can tell what they're thinking—what's happened to quiet little Izzy? Well, maybe I've got fed up with her. Since Grace took Mia on, Mia's shut up. No more of the snide comments, which I pretended not to hear, or the stupid posts on my timeline that I tried to ignore. But hoping it would all go away wasn't enough. It didn't work. It's the same with this.

"Sorry, Izzy, I shouldn't be defeatist," admits Dee, trying to smile. I can see she's also taken aback by my outburst. "You're right. It's always important to stand up for what you believe in. It's just that sometimes it feels like no one wants to listen. Now, come on, it's a big day, and if we sit around chatting anymore we're *all* going to be late."

Chapter Twenty-Four

As Megan and I walk past a bodega on the way to school, I can't help glancing at the headlines on the piles of papers outside. I watch the people coming out of the shop, wondering what they'll think when they open their papers today.

At school, I'm on edge, worried that other people might have seen that headline, too. I've got used to everyone going silent when I come into the classroom, or those little "accidental" jostles in the corridor from Lucas and Charlie and the others. But since Grace told Mia off at rehearsal, no one's actually *said* anything.

I haven't talked to Grace since Friday's rehearsal. She's still sitting with Olivia, but I feel like things could be okay, one day, even if I don't quite know how.

The morning whizzes by, especially since we know we're going to be let out of afternoon classes for the final rehearsal. It's so near the end of the year that none of the teachers are setting much homework. Even the sternest teachers, like Mrs. Dalton, seem more relaxed. She has us playing math games and doing Christmas-themed problems.

By the time it gets to last lesson of the morning—English with Mr. Thomas—I've almost forgotten about the conversation over breakfast.

"Right, seventh grade," says Mr. Thomas. "Just because it's nearly the end of term doesn't mean you can all slack off and stop working. Okay? There'll be plenty of time for that over the holidays. We're going to work hard today, and—" he pauses "—you'll be delighted to know, I've got some more fascinating homework for you tonight."

There's a chorus of groans. "But that's not fair. What about the play?" says Grace. "We won't have time to rehearse *and* do homework, Mr. Thomas."

"I know *some* of you are in the play," he continues, "and even if you're not, I hope *all* of you will be in the audience. Tickets are on sale, as I *think* I've mentioned once or twice before, in the office and on the school website." A couple of people laugh. Mr. Thomas has been harping on about ticket sales for weeks.

"But, never fear, this is homework that builds on our topics of journalistic and persuasive writing, *and* allows you to choose what to write about, so no one should have any problems with this one. We're going to be writing letters to the editor," says Mr. Thomas. "Who can tell me what a letter to the editor is?"

A few hands go up.

"It's in a newspaper," says Sheetal, "when they publish letters from their readers."

"That's right, so why might someone write a letter to the editor?"

"Because they want to complain."

"Because they want to say they like something."

"Because they think someone's wrong or been overlooked."

"Because they agree with what it says."

"Excellent. All good reasons. So, here's what I want you to do." He lifts his voice above the clamor. "You need to find an article in a newspaper or online, about any topic you like, and write a letter to the editor in response. Your letters need to be short, reference the original article, and make at least two points to back up your argument, and they need to be on my desk tomorrow morning." He holds up his hand. "People—no more groaning. Remember, news is only news when it's new. Today's papers will be old news by tomorrow."

"Now, we're going to look at some letters from yesterday's papers. In pairs, pick out and highlight where the writers use persuasive language. These phrases are going to help you to do your homework later. Charlie— can you hand these out, please?"

Today's papers will be old news by tomorrow. Really, is that what Mr. Thomas thinks? I hope he's right.

Chapter Twenty-Five

The dress rehearsal is part brilliant, part chaos. Mr. Thomas seems pleased and the whole cast is buzzing with excitement. Afterward, we hang up our costumes carefully on the racks, so we'll know where to find them quickly tomorrow night, wipe off our makeup, and leave Mr. Thomas to lock up the studio.

It's dark by the time we get out of school. There's a fine drizzle. Streetlights are reflected in the puddles on the pavement. I'm so tired that the last thing I feel like doing is my homework. I just want to curl up under my duvet, switch my brain off, and watch what Mom calls "trash TV."

When I come through the door, I see Dee sitting at the kitchen table. She must have got home early from work.

She looks like she's waiting for someone or something. Turns out it's me.

"Hey, Izzy. How'd it go? Are you all ready for opening night tomorrow?"

"Uh huh. I think so. I got all my words right anyway."

"Well done." She smiles. "Hot chocolate? I was just going to make myself a drink. . . ."

I nod, and slump down onto one of the kitchen chairs, resting my bag on the table and my head on my bag. "Make sure it's got four spoons in, though," I momble. "Really chocolatey."

"One super-luxury, extra-special, four-spoon hot chocolate just for you," she says, and puts my mug down in front of me with a flourish.

Then she's up and down out of her chair, fiddling with her spoon as she sugars her tea, drumming her fingers on the table. All the kinds of twitchy things that I do when I'm nervous about something.

"I spoke to Vicky earlier," she says, trying to sound casual. "She says good luck for tomorrow, by the way."

"Thanks," I mutter, licking the chocolatey sweetness from around my lips.

"We also talked about this article, you know, the one in the paper this morning?"

I nod. It's been on my mind all day, especially since Mr. Thomas's English lesson on letters to the editor. In fact, I've already started composing in my mind the letter that I'd want to write in response.

"Well, actually, not just about the article. You see, she had a phone call from someone from a local TV station, wanting to do a follow-up piece on the story with a local angle. For the TV. They asked her if anyone from the group would be willing to go on their breakfast show tomorrow to—what did she say?—'debate the issues.' Only for five minutes or so."

"So is she going to do it?" I ask. I can imagine Vicky with her smart clothes and rich voice in front of the camera, not letting anyone get the better of her. She'd be brilliant.

"No," says Dee slowly. "She'd like to, but, well, she might not look it and she might not act it, but she's had some hard times. She still gets very anxious about speaking in front of people. Do you know what I mean, Izzy?"

I remember what Vicky said in the garden about really being shy, and wanting her drawing to do the talking for her.

"So what are they going to do?" I ask. "Find someone else?"

Dee goes quiet and looks at me nervously, like she's

worried about what I'm going to say. And then I know.

"You?"

Another pause.

"Yes."

"But why you? Isn't there someone else? Like, someone who's been, you know, like this, for longer? Can't you find someone else?" I can hear the whine in my voice. I sound like Jamie when he doesn't want to eat his peas.

"But, Izzy, I want to do this. I do," she insists. "No one's making me do it. And it's not because there's no one else. It was you who inspired me actually—what you said at breakfast. I don't want to embarrass you or Megan. I didn't know what you'd say or how you'd feel. But I remembered what you'd said earlier. You're right, when something isn't fair it *is* important to stand up for what you believe in."

But that wasn't what I meant at all. Not her. Not now. Not like this in front of everyone.

"And there's one more thing. . . ." She looks down at her hands, resting on the table. "I'd like you to come with me. No, not to be on TV, of course not," she says quickly, registering my shocked face. "But just to come along for the ride, be there, with me. It would be nice to have someone, a friendly face, that's all. You're always so calm. It would be a bit of an early start but. . . ." She trails off.

"No. No, I won't come with you. How can you even ask me? Tomorrow's *my* day. My day. Mine. Not yours." My voice is shrill. I'm getting louder and louder.

"But, Izzy, come on, calm down, sweetheart, this isn't like you."

"No, I won't calm down. I won't. Don't you realize? Everyone will see you. And they'll laugh. It's bad enough as it is. You're not there when people say horrible stuff at school or when they whisper about me behind my back because of you. You don't know what it's like. This will just make everything even worse."

I run out of the kitchen and slam the door behind me. I don't want to see Dee's shocked face anymore. I stumble up the stairs and into my room.

Chapter Twenty-Six

I'm shaking and my knees feel weak, but I can't sit still. I pace up and down the room.

The same thoughts keep going round and round in my head: How can she be serious about doing this? She doesn't even look like a proper woman yet. How can I go into school after that? And what's worse, it's *my* first night. How can she be so selfish?

Perhaps Megan will talk her out of it. But then all Megan can think about now is her art competition. Maybe Mom will? I can't imagine she'd want all her private business talked about on TV.

There's a light knock on my door.

I don't answer.

If it's Dee, I don't want to see her. I crawl into bed, head under the duvet, my face to the wall.

"Izzy?" says Mom's voice gently, and she pushes the door slowly open. I stay silent.

Mom sits at the end of the bed. She puts her hand awkwardly on my shoulder.

When I don't respond, she takes it away again and just sits in silence for a little while.

I'm sure as hell not going to be the first one to talk. I've got nothing to say to either of them.

"Izzy, I know you're angry."

No prizes for detective work there.

"It's okay to be angry. I know it's hard for you, all of this. You've been so good about it all, we should have known it was all going to come out some time. It's been a lot to ask."

I don't move. I just lie there, waiting for her to go away and leave me alone.

"You know, I get angry, too," sighs Mom. "Even if I don't show it. Not angry with you, sweetheart, but with your dad, and with myself and with how people are, the whole damn situation.

"This might all have been a big surprise for you, but I always knew. I always knew, right from when your dad and I first got together, even if we didn't have the words to talk about it. But we thought love would be enough. We were in love. We got married. I got pregnant with Megan. We thought that would be the cure, I suppose. I should have said all of this before. I should have explained."

It's unsettling hearing Mom talk like this, about her and Dad before I was born. When I was little I used to love hearing the story of my birth—the rush to the hospital through the February snow, the midwife saying what a big, beautiful baby I was, Megan helping Gran bake a birthday cake for when Mom and Dad brought me home. But I never liked stories from before then so much. It felt too odd to imagine a world without me in it. A world in which, if something had happened differently, I might not have even existed.

"But it's not a disease," continues Mom. "Being trans isn't something you have to cure or change. We couldn't have anyway, however long we tried. It took the two of us years to work that out. We're still working it all out now, just without any more secrets from you." She stops for a moment and lowers her voice. "It's not been easy. I still worry sometimes if we're doing the right thing. I hate the idea of people gossiping about us, or making thoughtless comments, or the thought that this will make life harder for you, Megan, or Jamie. I'm your mom. All I want to do is protect you.

"But don't think it's been the only thing in our lives,

there's been so much else to think about, like seeing you three grow up and make us so proud. We should have realized, if it took us so long, it was bound to take you a while to get used to how things are changing, too."

It's not often Mom makes such a long speech. Even when she's telling us off or congratulating us for something, she usually keeps it short.

"So, Izzy, what I'm saying is, you don't have to get up early tomorrow and traipse into some TV studio not far from Boston and be all smiles. I know you've got a big few days ahead. I told her that she shouldn't ask you, but you know how she is when she gets onto an idea." There's a smile in her voice. "I think we're all a bit stubborn in this family."

I relax a little bit. I think she can tell somehow, even if I don't move or say anything, because she seems to relax, too. The atmosphere in the room is less stifling. At least Mom's on my side.

Then there's the "but."

"But you can't stop her doing it. Believe me, I've tried." Mom pauses, sighs again. "It will be okay, you know, I promise."

Mom's finished speaking. All I can hear is the clock ticking and the whir of the washing machine from the kitchen below.

Eventually I feel her get off the bed and hear her padding to the door. She shuts it gently behind her.

I don't know how long I lie there for. It seemed like Mom understood, but how she can be so sure it will all be okay? She won't be the one that everyone will be staring at in school tomorrow.

I get out my phone and start writing a long message to Grace about my parents and how awful they are, and about Dee going on TV and how I'll never live it down. Just writing the words makes me feel much better. There's no one else who'd understand how I'm feeling. No one else I'd want to tell.

Anyway, I don't have to send it.

It's late by now. I can hear Mom and Dee's voices as they come upstairs on their way to bed. I put my ear to the door, so that I can hear when they've gone. I'm not quite ready to face them yet.

I can only make out the odd word. Then Mom's voice, suddenly louder as they pass my door: "Enough about standing up for what you believe in. You're not Martin Luther King. Save it for the TV cameras." But she doesn't sound angry. There's a warmth and a chuckle in her voice. Dee laughs and murmurs something I can't hear.

The whole house is dark except for a small slither of

light under Megan's door. I sneak downstairs, raid the fridge for what I can find, and tiptoe back upstairs with my own private midnight feast.

My phone's still on my bedside table, message to Grace waiting.

I press SEND.

Chapter Twenty-Seven

I'm onstage in the school auditorium. The stage lights are bright and the audience is shrouded in darkness. The band strikes up. I open my mouth and start singing.

But the music is playing far too fast and all the wrong words are coming out of my mouth. The audience begin to shuffle in their seats. Then they start throwing things at the stage. I duck out of the way, and all I can hear is the patter of tiny objects landing all around me.

I wake up, covered in sweat and tangled up in my duvet. The bedside clock is flashing 5:47. Thank god.

But the pattering sound continues. It's coming from outside my window. I leap out of bed, trip over the plate with the remains of my late-night snack, and pull back the curtains.

It's dark and wet outside. Hard to see anything in the street below. Then another smattering sound. Someone is throwing something at my window.

I open the window and look down.

"Hey, what are you doing?" I shout.

"At last!" Grace shouts back. "Let me in, it's freezing out here."

Oh my god, it is. It's Grace. She looks real enough, standing there in the rain, but maybe I am still dreaming.

I creep downstairs, although I don't know why—we've already made enough noise to wake up half the street. There's a light on in the kitchen. I unlock the front door and Grace bounds in, her coat dripping.

"What on earth are you doing here?" I say sleepily, wrapping my robe round me more tightly. "And what were you throwing at my window?"

"Just gravel," says Grace. "I read about it in a book. I thought it would be a good way to attract your attention without waking up anyone else. But you took ages to come to the window, and it was so wet out there. And, oh, Izzy, I'm sorry. I'm so, so sorry."

She enfolds me in a huge, damp hug. "I've been a terrible friend. I've been so stupid. I got your message last night and I couldn't sleep. I just had to come and help."

"Okay, okay, stop it, you're dripping all over me." I push her gently away. I feel like I'm still half asleep and must be dreaming. "I don't get it. What are you doing here so early?"

"I could ask the same question," says a puzzled voice behind me. "Although of course it's always lovely to see you, Grace, it is a *little* bit early."

"Hello, Danielle," says Grace, suddenly cheerful again. "You look great. Very stylish, but not too over the top. Just right for TV."

Dee's standing in the kitchen doorway, holding a cup of tea. I have to agree with Grace, her clothes and her hair do look good. It's just her face that's deathly pale, even with the makeup.

"Er . . . okay." Dee's still looking puzzled, but my sleepy brain is slowly working out what Grace's doing here.

"You see," Grace continues, "we figured—me and Izzy—we thought that perhaps you'd need some moral support on your way to the TV studios. We can do that. We wouldn't be any trouble. We'd just be there to, you know, keep your spirits up, distract you from getting too nervous."

My mouth opens and shuts, but no words come out.

Dee raises an eyebrow. "Did you now, Grace? And did

213

you happen to mention any of this to your mom?"

"We-e-ll..." Grace stretches the word out as long as she can. "Not exactly."

"No, I thought not. It's a very kind thought, Grace, but I can't drive you off across the county and maybe make you late for school without permission from your mom. She'll be worried sick. Sorry."

She looks over at me, but I can't meet her eyes. "Anyway, I'm not sure that Izzy wants to come, do you, love?"

"Oh, I'm sure she does," Grace says quickly. "She wouldn't want to miss this. Don't worry about my mom, I left her a note. And she gets up really early. I bet you could text her now and make sure it will all be okay."

"Hmm . . ." says Dee thoughtfully. "Izzy, what do you think?"

I look up. Two pairs of pleading eyes are looking directly at me.

"All right then," I say. Grace gives a little squeal of delight. Dee smiles at me. What seemed so dreadful last night doesn't seem so bad this morning. It could even be fun, now that Grace is coming, too.

"Come on, quick, you need to get some clothes on. Your hair's a mess. When do we have to leave?"

"Ten minutes," says Dee, checking her watch. "And,

Grace, this is only if I get through to speak to your mom, okay? Don't wake up Jamie by thundering up the stairs—he's got school today, and a late night with the show tonight."

I think that's a bit unfair. After all, *I've* got school, *and* a late night at the show, too. But I let Grace drag me upstairs to get ready as Dee shuts the kitchen door gently behind her to phone Mrs. Okafor in peace.

"What are you doing here?" I hiss. "I thought we weren't even friends. And even if we *are* friends again—didn't you *read* my message? This is a disaster. I don't want her going on TV. If she does, the last thing I want to do is go with her. I don't want to be right there when she makes a fool of herself!"

"You dummy! Of *course* you want to go, and you want to take me. It's a real TV studio, with all the lights and cameras and makeup. And your dad's going to be on TV. And she needs us. It'll be like having a celebrity in your family. No one I know's *ever* been on TV before. Oh my god, we might even meet someone famous."

"It's the *local news*. It's not Hollywood. We're not going to bump into any film stars, just washed-out old local newscasters."

"But it's still a real TV studio. How cool will that be?

We might never get the chance again. Not till I'm a film star myself. Think about it, Izzy."

"I *am* thinking about it. I'm thinking about my dad making a laughingstock of me. My dad, Grace, my dad in a dress. On TV. And everyone watching."

But even as I try to explain how I feel to Grace, I realize that I don't mean what I'm saying anymore. I don't feel as upset, like the world's going to end, as I did yesterday. Instead of imagining how awful it will be, I think of all the people who won't laugh—like Megan's friends, or Sam, or Mr. Thomas—the people who'll just accept Dee for who she is, who'll listen to what she has to say.

And then there's Grace. She's already made me feel better, like anything's possible and everything's an adventure. It feels unreal that we're friends again, and yet the most natural thing in the world, too.

Now that I feel better, it's up to me to make Dee feel better, too. Yes, I needed Grace, but right now, Dee needs me. Of course she does. I've got to be there. I can't let her down.

"Let's go, Izzy, come on, don't change your mind, pretty please."

Grace makes her eyes go all big, tilts her head to one

side, and clasps her hands together. She looks so pitiful that it makes me laugh.

Then she starts laughing, too. And we find we can't stop. Soon my stomach hurts and I'm gasping for air. It feels so good.

I know that nothing my dad says or does is going to make Grace any less my friend. I know that all that stuff with Sam is way behind us now.

We stifle our laughter behind our hands, so as not to disturb Jamie, and bundle into my room. In less than ten minutes, I'm dressed in my school uniform, hair up, teeth brushed, and ready to go.

Dee's waiting by the door, jangling the car keys. All she says is, "Your mother is a very understanding woman, Grace," and then we're off.

I shovel all the old chips packets, coloring pens, and hair bands that cover the back seat into a pile on Jamie's car seat on one side, and Grace and I squash together on the other. The car radio's on low. I can tell Dee's nervous, despite looking so poised, by the way she keeps chattering away about nothing as we weave our way through the outskirts of town and onto the main road. I'm sure she's glad we're here. I'm so relieved. Thanks to Grace, I made the right decision after all.

It's still so quiet outside. The roads are almost empty. Just a couple of women huddled under their umbrellas, waiting for the early bus. Rush hour hasn't started yet, so only the occasional car swooshes past in the other direction. Butterflies are fluttering in my stomach. I'm nervous and excited all at once. I also suddenly realize that I'm ravenously hungry—why didn't I grab some breakfast before I left?

Just before we leave town, Dee points out a street of old houses. "Having you two here reminds me. I was down there a few weeks ago for a job. The plans for some attic extension. Nice house, all original features."

Yawn. Dee will talk about houses and fireplaces and features all day if anyone listens. Even if they don't.

"Nice family, too, Pearce, I think they were, their son's at St. Mary's. I'd recognize the uniform anywhere. We had a nice chat about the school. I think he's in your show, too, you probably know him."

"Pearce?!" Grace and I say at exactly the same time. We're so surprised that we don't even jinx.

"Not Lucas Pearce?" I say. Grace makes a gagging sound.

"I think so," says Dee. "Yes, Lucas sounds familiar. Polite lad. Do you know him?"

"Yeah," says Grace, rolling her eyes. "Yeah, we know

him." She leans over to me and whispers, "Lucas? Polite? What an act. If only he was that good in *Guys and Dolls*!"

I gasp. This means one thing: It must have been Lucas who told everyone at school about Dee all along. Not Megan's friends and not Grace. Not that I ever thought it was, not really. But now I can be sure.

That makes me feel even more terrible about doubting Grace in the first place. What if she remembers those awful things I said and decides she shouldn't have made up with me after all?

I shoot her an anxious glance. "I'm sorry, too," I whisper.

She grins back and squeezes my hand, but she looks worried too underneath her smile. "That's okay. I shouldn't have said what I did. I didn't mean it, any of it," she says.

"I know, me neither. I was worried you'd never want to be my friend again."

She stares past me, out of the window. "I've been so miserable these last two weeks," she sighs quietly. "Let's not fall out again, whatever happens. Okay?"

"Hand on heart."

"Hand on heart," she echoes. "Do you think we can forget all about it and be friends just like before?"

I stop. "No," I say thoughtfully. "No, I don't think we can forget about it. It will always have happened, won't it? But it can still be okay. We're still best friends, aren't we?"

"Too right!" says Grace happily. "It's been so boring hanging out with Olivia, you wouldn't believe. It's always much more fun with you. Here—" she starts rummaging in her pockets "—look what I've got!"

She pulls out a slightly squashed Kit Kat, peels off the wrapper, snaps it in half, and hands me a piece. "I've been saving it," she says and smiles.

"This is it," says Dee, suddenly swerving into an almost deserted parking lot. "We're here."

Chapter Twenty-Eight

The TV studios are in a huge glass building. All windows, blazing lights, and giant revolving doors. I instinctively reach for Dee's hand, even though I'm far too old for holding hands, and we go in together.

Grace is soaking it all up, scrutinizing the people as they go past: some in suits, most in jeans and jackets, almost all with important-looking ID cards swinging around their necks and cups of coffee in their hands.

"Hello, hello, good morning, you must be Danielle?" says a brisk blonde woman with impossibly bright lipstick and a glinting gold stud in her nose. Without waiting for Dee to reply, she rattles on. "I'm Ellie, your producer? Thank you so much for coming in on such a miserable morning? It was me you spoke to on the phone?" Everything

Ellie says sounds like a question, so it's hard to know when, if ever, she might actually expect you to reply.

"You're on time, no rush at all, so we'll just head up to the green room and meet the other guests?"

"Is it still all right for my daughter and her friend to come up, too?" says Dee apologetically, as Ellie strides off toward the elevators. "I probably should have called over to check, but everything happened very suddenly."

Ellie turns to look at Grace and me. We must look very young, standing there in our school uniforms. I hadn't even thought that they might not let us in. For once, even Grace is silent.

Ellie beams at us with the most enormous smile. "Well, we wouldn't normally," she says, "but let's make an exception for the two of you, shall we? You look like very grown-up, sensible girls. You must be excited to see your da— uh, your mu— uh, well, Danielle, on the TV?"

We squeeze into the elevator, and then Ellie leads us through a maze of corridors, using her ID card to open door after door. It's so confusing, I'd never get out of this place by myself.

Then one last door opens into a small room with comfy seats and a small table in the middle. A bit like

222

a fancy doctor's waiting room.

"This must be the green room," whispers Grace.

Ellie finds us three chairs and offers us all tea. Only Dee says yes, and then a second later changes her mind.

"Now," says Ellie firmly but still at breakneck speed, reeling off details she knows by heart, "you've seen the program before, haven't you?" Dee nods. "Your segment is just eight minutes or so, and it'll go in a flash. There's nothing to worry about. Kevin Doherty will introduce the issue, why it's in the news today, we'll play a short clip, and then he'll ask you and our other guest some questions to get a local response. All good? You've got about ten minutes till we go live. Someone from makeup will be here in a sec, just to give you a little touch-up, okay?"

Dee nods. Grace nods, too.

I nudge her. "Not for you, you dope."

"I know," she says, smiling. "Exciting, though, isn't it?"

I have to admit she's right. I look around. There's a huge screen on the wall where you can see what's on TV right now, and framed pictures of past guests and presenters. I vaguely recognize some of them, although I wouldn't know their names. It's weird to think that in ten minutes we'll be sitting here, watching Dee on that same screen.

I glance over at Dee, and guess she's thinking the same thing. "Nervous?" I whisper. There are only a couple of other people in the room, and they're deep in conversation, but I still feel like I shouldn't talk too loud.

"A little," she says and squeezes my hand.

"You'll be great. You will."

I try to think of something to say to make her feel better. Finally, I remember what Mr. Thomas told me the other day about Adele. So, while a woman with a pouch full of brushes and powder sets to work on Dee's face, I rattle on about how even the most experienced performers get stage fright, and how she should take deep breaths to help her stay calm.

Suddenly Grace grabs my arm.

"Oh my god. What's *he* doing here?"

Grace tilts her head toward the door. A tall man with a dark blue suit and broad shoulders has just walked in.

"Who's that?" I whisper back. But before she can answer, the tall man walks right over to us and greets Grace warmly.

"Miss Grace Okafor," he booms. "How are you, young lady? What a pleasant surprise."

"Morning, Pastor," says Grace quietly, fiddling with her braids.

And then I realize, it's him. Pastor Johnson from Grace's church. The man who thinks my dad is an abomination.

Chapter Twenty-Nine

"What are you doing here, Grace?" asks Pastor Johnson. "Is your mother here, too? Hmm?" He looks over her school uniform. "This isn't exactly on your way to school."

Then he notices me and Dee, reaching out to shake Dee's hand, and mine. It is the firmest handshake I've ever had. I can feel my fingers tingling afterward.

"Pastor Johnson," he says, in a voice as firm as the handshake. "Pleased to meet you . . ." Perhaps I'm just imagining the flicker of distaste in his eyes as looks at Dee.

"Danielle Palmer," says Dee, "and this is my daughter Isabel. You know Grace already, I see."

Ellie bustles over, headset on and clipboard in hand. "Good, good," she gushes. "Have you two met each other already? Isn't it good that you've had a chat before you go on? It makes the interview so much more natural. Pastor, Danielle, the weather's just starting, so it's time for you to go on any second now. How about I take you through and get you settled." She waves at Grace and me. "See you later, girls!"

"What is *he* doing here?" I say to Grace.

"Search me. Did you see he was wearing makeup?"

"Of course he was, you dolt, he's about to go on TV. Everyone wears makeup in front of the—" I'm suddenly short of breath, as my ears and my brain and my mouth all catch up with each other in a rush. "Grace! He's going to be on TV, too. With Dee. The wearing-women's-clothes-is-an-abomination pastor."

And now I know what's going on, and there's nothing I can do about it.

". . . That's all for the weather this morning. Have a good day—and don't forget your umbrellas!" chirps the weatherman from the screen on the wall.

Grace and I move closer to the TV, as the camera zooms in on Dee, Pastor Johnson, and Kevin Doherty, the presenter. They are all sitting along a pastel green sofa, pretending to be comfortable and relaxed. The TV station logo looms behind them.

227

I've only seen the program a few times, mostly when I've been home from school sick with nothing else to do, but it's still surreal seeing Dee on the TV.

"Welcome to our Local Look part of the program," beams Kevin.

He's barely said more than a couple of words and I'm already finding him really irritating. My mouth is dry. I swallow hard and wish I'd said yes to Ellie's offer of tea.

"Local Look is where we get the local angle on one of the week's headline stories," continues Kevin. "Yesterday's report from the Institute of Gender Studies got people talking when it revealed that increasing numbers of children are attending gender clinics. A worrying sign or a welcome development? We have with us in the studio Danielle Palmer from TransAnglia, a support group bringing together transgender people from across the region—" Grace and I exchange glances, as Dee says good morning "—and Jerome Johnson from the New Life Redeemed Church. But first, here's our report."

As a prerecorded clip starts playing, Grace turns to me and says earnestly, "She's doing all right, isn't she? I mean, she's doing well."

"Grace, all she's done is sit on a sofa. And say hello. They haven't even asked her any questions yet."

"Yeah, but she looks relaxed. Not like earlier. Honestly, Izzy, she looked so off that I thought she was going to puke, right there in reception."

"Sssh," I hiss. "She's back on now."

Kevin turns his smile on Dee. "Let's start with you, Danielle, do you think it's right that gender clinics are now full of very young children wanting to change their gender? I mean, shouldn't we just let children be children?" he simpers.

"Come on, come on, come on," I mutter under my breath. *Please don't mess this up. Please be okay. Please.*

"Well, first of all, Kevin, that's simply not true," says Dee calmly, all her nerves seemingly gone. "No one is suggesting that children undergo any kind of inappropriate treatment. All this report is saying is that we should be listening to our children, something I'm sure we can all agree on. Ignoring the situation isn't going to make it go away. I should know."

"Go, Danielle!" squeals Grace, jumping up and down. "What a great answer!"

"Ah, yes," Kevin continues, "I believe you have children of your own, Danielle. How are they coping with your transition? Surely there must have been some difficult questions. It's a lot for young children to take in, isn't it?"

"It's not been easy for me, coming to terms with who I really am. It's taken many years, and I've still got a long journey ahead. And it's not always easy for my family either...." She pauses and looks down for a moment. Only for a moment, but long enough for my stomach to sink into my shoes.

"My children understand what's going on and I'm proud of the support they've given me. I couldn't ask for a better family. But not every trans person has support from their families, friends, or employers, even their doctors— that's why this report is so important, showing simple ways to improve attitudes to trans people across the board."

Listening to Dee, part of me feels proud enough to burst: She is *killing* this interview. Another part wants to crawl away and hide. Those dreadful things I said last night. *Couldn't ask for a better family*? Yeah, right.

"I'd like to bring Pastor Johnson in here. You have a slightly different perspective, don't you?"

"That's right," he says in his deep, firm voice. "While I appreciate Danielle's experience, there are so many risks here."

"Did you hear?" hisses Grace, outraged. "He says 'Danielle,' like it's in inverted commas, not her real name!"

"We're meddling with something that we don't fully

230

understand. Just because we can now enable people to change their bodies in this way doesn't mean that we should do it. There are faith groups, women's organizations and many others who agree on that. We need caution."

"Caution's all very well," says Dee, leaning forward. "But while we're being cautious, how many young trans people are suffering? How many more are being bullied or harming themselves? That's what we should be addressing here. How to stop that problem. And we can't do that by saying that trans people shouldn't exist, or ignoring the fact they do. We can't do it by pretending that trans people aren't in our families, our schools, our workplaces...."

I wonder if Sam's watching at home, his dad watching, too, remembering what it was like when he was growing up.

"So, Danielle," cuts in Kevin, leaning toward her on the sofa, wrinkling his forehead to try and look concerned, "the issue that some of our viewers will be anxious about, and which this report raises, is that talking about these subjects with young children makes it, well, fashionable to be transgender. It confuses children and can lead to decisions that may be regretted later. That's not an unreasonable concern, is it?"

Pastor Johnson is nodding furiously.

Dee bites her lip and looks nervous. I shut my eyes and try to send positive thoughts her way, even though I know it won't make any difference.

After what feels like ages, she asks the other two, "Did you learn history at school?"

I open my eyes and see them both nodding tentatively. There's a close-up on Kevin, who looks slightly anxious, like he's not sure where this interview is going next.

Grace looks at me and mouths, "What?" I shrug.

"So, for example, is learning about the French Revolution at school going to encourage our children to chop off people's heads?" She pauses. "Of course not. Having a better understanding about trans people isn't going to make someone trans, but I hope it might make them a more tolerant person. Seeing only people who weren't trans around me as I was growing up didn't stop me being who I am. It just made it so much harder."

Suddenly I see how lonely it must have been for Dee when she was a kid, and later, even with Mom around, how invisible she must have felt. I know what that feels like, just a little. I feel a rush of gratitude that I've now got Grace, and Sam, too, I suppose, friends who understand me and who'll stick up for me. Despite how scared she must feel, Dee's up there where thousands of people can see, trying to help other people. Perhaps I need to stand up, too.

They keep talking for a bit longer—the pastor sounding calm and reasonable, but Dee giving as good as she gets. It seems like only a few seconds until it's all over, Kevin thanks them and the next item starts. I check my watch: It's not even time for breakfast yet.

Dee walks in through the green-room door, pale but smiling. Grace runs forwards to hug her, burbling, "I hope you don't mind, I just had to, I mean, wow." Dee hugs her back and looks at me over Grace's head. Her eyes are questioning. Waiting.

And then, I'm hugging her, too. And Grace. A strange hug sandwich with my dad and my best friend.

When my blazer pocket starts buzzing, I break free from the hug.

"Hey, Mom."

"Hi, Izzy, are you all right?" crackles Mom's voice on the other end of the line.

"Yes," I smile. "Yes, I'm fine."

"You didn't have to do this, you know, you could—"

"I know," I interrupt. "It's okay. I'll pass you over."

"Thanks, Izzy," she says, and I know that she's not just saying thank you for handing over the phone.

As Dee chats to Mom, and Jamie joins in, too, Pastor Johnson walks over to me and Grace.

"See you on Sunday?" he says quietly to Grace. She nods.

"You, too." He turns to me. "Any friend of Grace's would always be welcome at church."

For once, I find myself speaking without even thinking.

"And what about Dee? What about my dad? Would she be welcome, too?"

For a few seconds, there's an awkward silence. "Nothing I've heard today's going to change my mind," Pastor Johnson continues finally. "With God's help, I know the right way to live and that's what I'm called to help my church to follow. But as to being welcome, do you understand what I mean by 'love the sinner, hate the sin'? Everyone sins in different ways, but everyone's loved by God. Your family would be very welcome, Isabel."

Somehow, I'm not convinced.

Chapter Thirty

"What do you think's better—being on TV or being onstage?" says Grace through a mouthful of bacon roll. We stopped at a café on our way back to the car, all ravenous, and loaded up with the greasiest food we could find. I've wolfed all of mine down already.

"Being in a stage show," I say. "One hundred percent. You're with other people, aren't you? Not just the audience, I mean, but everyone else onstage, too. You're part of a team."

"Yeah, but you can get really famous on TV. More people can see you," she muses.

"I suppose so," I say, some of my joy fading.

"We're not even going to miss any school," grumbles

Grace, peering out of the window. "Look, we're back in town already and it's only quarter past eight."

"No point in going home, though," says Dee. "I'll drop you both by the gates, and then head to work."

"There's no need. . . ." I start to say, then realize that now thousands of people have seen Dee on TV this morning, there's no point in worrying if one or two people see us outside school.

Dee stops the car and leans back to look at us both. "Thanks, girls," she says. "That meant a lot to me, you being there. I know it sounds silly, but I honestly don't think I would have been brave enough otherwise."

"Our pleasure," replies Grace, with a little bow.

"Now, time to forget all about it and focus on tonight. *Your* big night," says Dee firmly. "Oh, and you remember today's the day that Megan's masterpiece goes up on display, don't you? She's probably already been in school for ages setting it up. Make sure you have a look and report back—I still don't know what on earth it's going to be."

Oh, yes, the art prize. I had forgotten that was today, too. Megan says all the artwork goes up for a week, and then the winner is announced in the final assembly at the end of school.

Stepping out of the car is like waking up from a dream

and finding yourself back in real life. One of those surreal dreams where there are people you know, but in places you don't, or they're doing things you don't expect.

This is definitely real life. People pouring through the gates, shoving, jostling, laughing, shouting, just another school day. Me, Isabel Palmer, only a tiny part of a huge crowd. Almost unnoticed.

"Hey, Izzy, hey, Grace," says a voice behind us. Sam. How does he always manage to appear out of nowhere? He puts an arm around each of our shoulders, and we carry on walking, the three of us together.

"Hey, Sam," says Grace, beaming. "You'll never guess what we've been doing this morning."

By now, Sam's spent enough rehearsal time with Grace to know that she's always got a dramatic story to tell.

"Go on then, spill it."

"Well." She pauses for effect. "Did you see Izzy's dad on TV this morning?"

"Grace," I hiss. "Shhh."

"Serious?" says Sam, turning to me. "Your dad was on TV, Izzy, no lie?"

I nod. I suppose telling Sam about it is okay. He looks impressed; surprised, puzzled, but definitely impressed.

"You know Local Look?" continues Grace.

"With that smarmy guy with dyed hair on the sofa?"

237

asks Sam.

"Uh huh. Izzy's dad was one of the guests. She let us go in with her, we saw everything, all the behind-the-scenes stuff. A real TV studio."

"She was on TV, talking about . . . ?" says Sam, still looking at me.

"Yes," I reply quickly.

Sam whistles. "That's brave. My dad would never dream of doing anything like . . ." He freezes. I can see from his eyes that he's worried he might have given away something about his dad in front of Grace.

Just at that moment, the bell rings. Sam shoots off in one direction—"See you later, see you tonight!"—and Grace and I dash off in the other, her arm hooked into mine.

"Oh my god, I can still feel his arm over my shoulders. I'll never let my mom wash my blazer again!" she squeals. "But what was he going on about his dad for? Why would anyone ask *Sam's* dad to be on TV?"

Chapter Thirty-One

There's a bit of whispering and nudging in the classroom as Grace and I go in and find our seats. That's no different from normal, though. I still don't know if anyone's actually seen the breakfast show this morning.

But I do start to relax. Who watches breakfast TV anyway? And even if they do, are they even going to know that's my dad? Palmer's a common enough name after all. And then a new thought strikes me, even if they did know, would I even care? Dee was brilliant this morning. Why should it matter what anyone else thinks?

It's so good to be sitting next to Grace again, for the first time in ages, that I barely notice everyone else rummaging in their bags as Mr. Thomas comes in. I suddenly realize—homework. Even Grace's done hers. She clicks open her sticker-covered, pink binder and pulls out a sheet of paper. I've just got a blank sheet. Maybe he won't notice, and I can slip mine into the marking pile tomorrow.

"Right, seventh grade," says Mr. Thomas, looking around. "I hope everyone's got their letters to the editor ready. Instead of handing them in now, we're going to hear some of them read aloud. Then we can all comment on the quality of the persuasive writing."

"Is it cos you can't be bothered to mark them, sir?" calls out Lucas.

"Ah, Lucas, what an incisive comment," says Mr. Thomas. "It looks like you're first up. Thank you for volunteering. Don't be shy, come and join me at the front."

Lucas shuffles up to the front of the classroom, coughs a bit, and then starts reading. After Lucas's letter—a passionate condemnation of one paper's biased football coverage—comes Sheetal, something about climate change and the importance of saving the planet. Then Olivia, a suggestion that this paper should print more photos of cute kittens. Mr. Thomas rolls his eyes, but tells her how good her writing is and how if he was the editor, he'd definitely have more space devoted to kittens. Olivia glows.

"Well done, all, I'm really impressed. Good use of language, good choice of topics. Now, who's next?" I fix my eyes on my desk, hoping that he won't notice me.

But no luck. "Let's see, Isabel, will you come up and read your letter for us?"

"I didn't do it," I hiss to Grace.

"What? You *always* do your homework," she whispers back.

"Not this time. I just forgot."

"Well, you're just going to have to make something up...." she says, giving me a little shove to get me out of my seat. I feel sick and shaky. I hate getting into trouble.

Mr. Thomas looks at me questioningly, as I walk to the front of the class.

I stand there for a moment, looking at everyone's faces, bored or tired or simply getting ready to listen.

I wonder what role I'm going to play here and now, what kind of performance everyone is expecting. Today, I'm not Sarah Brown, lead in *Guys and Dolls*, just plain old Isabel Palmer. But which Isabel Palmer? Star of the show or the girl nobody notices? Best friend or social outcast? The daughter who's proud of her family or the one who's so embarrassed she wishes she could crawl under the table and hide?

"So, er, okay," I start nervously. I try desperately to remember the letter that I started writing in my head on my way home last night.

"Dear Sir," I begin. "I am writing about your article—'Grammar School Kids Forced into Sex Change.' I was very sad to read this article. Firstly, because the headline is not true: Children aren't forced to change their gender. Secondly, because lots of people find the words 'sex change' offensive. Thirdly, because lots of transgender people get bullied and it would be better to write an article against bullying in your paper instead of this one. I hope you will print an apology and write a new article, where you talk to people who can share their own experience. Yours faithfully, Isabel Palmer."

There's silence. No one is shuffling in their seats or looking bored anymore, instead they are all looking at me.

"Actually, Mr. Thomas, can I say something else?" I continue, my mouth saying the words before my brain's properly caught up. He nods, surprised, but it doesn't matter because I'm not really asking. Now I'm up here I know I'm just going to keep on talking.

I take a deep breath. I know what I want to say, but what if I say the wrong thing or, worse, the words don't come out at all?

"It's about something that's been happening this year, and about something that started happening before I was even born."

I look up at the class. Everything's a blur except two faces. Grace is smiling at me and giving me a thumbs-up. And, right at the back, there's Sam, looking at me seriously, intently, like he's willing me on.

"Most of you know about my dad. It's not like it's a secret, not anymore. I've heard the comments and the jokes." I pause, slow down. I've never heard the class this quiet before. "My dad is trans. She says she's taken years and years to be able to start living the way she wants to, but now she is. And although that totally confuses me, and I don't understand it, and most of the time I don't like it, it's something that's true.

"This morning she went on TV to talk about what that's like, because of this article in the paper which printed lies about people like her, the one I wrote my letter about. Someone asked her to do it, and she said yes because it was the right thing to do. Maybe you saw it, maybe not. But thousands of people did, and probably judged her on how she looked, or made comments about what she said. But she still said what she wanted to say, and maybe it helped someone. What you look like or what gender you are, or any of that, it's nobody's business but yours. You should just say what you want to say and stand up for the right thing. That's all."

From what seems like miles away, Mr. Thomas says something to me and then to the class, the bell goes and people clear their desks. A couple of people touch my shoulder on their way out, or whisper, "Thanks, Izzy," or, "That was so cool."

I don't move. I'm still shaking, but not because I'm scared. Instead I feel alive. Like I'm filled up with power and crackling with energy. Because, after all, what's there really to be scared of now?

Chapter Thirty-Two

66 **Y**ou two, my leading ladies, come with me," says Mr. Thomas, once the classroom is almost empty. "I've got something to show you—that's if you don't mind giving up five minutes of your break." He steers Grace and me gently down the corridor. "You've been so busy this morning, I guess you haven't had time to see the art exhibition yet. Come on, there's something I'll think you'll want to see."

He pushes open the doors to the hall. Normally just dark wood walls and rows of scuffed chairs, today it is transformed into a blaze of color and a world of weirdness.

Hanging from the ceiling is a vast shimmering bird made of tissue paper and, glinting in the sunlight from the long windows, barbed wire.

245

"Hmm . . ." says Mr. Thomas, following my gaze. "I'm not sure how they got that one through the front door." There are huge canvases hung on one wall, screens with flickering images, and a case of tiny delicate wire sculptures nestled in one corner. I'd never thought before there were so many people, even just in St. Mary's, who were so good at making things.

Right in front of me is the loudest and most in-your-face object in the whole room. Somehow, even though I don't know for sure that she made it, it shouts "Megan" right at me. It's an enormous pot, easily big enough for Jamie to hide in, that looks like it's made from papier-mâché. It's a deep, vivid red, with stark black lettering: *GET OVER IT.*

But up close, you can see that it's not solid blocks of color at all. The red and black are made up of photos, newspaper cuttings, words and images—some I recognize, most I don't. They come from magazines, our own family photos, images and articles I read online while trying to find out what being trans was really all about. I recognize some from Mom's list of websites. Some are stats, some are quotes from celebrities, some are just words by themselves. All the words and images are about prejudice, no, not that, they are all about different kinds of people and groups who get picked on. But somehow Megan's made them all look strong, not like victims at all.

The detail is immense. She must have spent hours pulling all this together. I reach out and touch it, tracing the rough surface with my fingertips. Hard and yet delicate at the same time. I'm sure Megan wouldn't mind.

"Not bad, is it?" says Mr. Thomas, walking up behind me. I can hear the smile in his voice. "You come from a pretty special family, Isabel." Based on everything that's happened so far this morning, I have to agree. "Don't forget how special you are," he continues softly. "How brave you can be, and how your bravery can help other people, too, to be open, to be brave themselves. I hope I'll get to meet your dad at the show tonight, and your mom— she must be quite something, too."

"I hope you will, too," I say, and I'm not just saying it, I really mean it. For the first time, the feeling of dread has lifted and I'm looking forward to Dee coming to the show tonight. "They're all coming. My little brother as well. He's really excited."

"I'm bringing someone special tonight, too," he replies. "Lewis—he's, er—" Mr. Thomas coughs "—he's my partner. He hasn't been to anything at the school before, but I couldn't resist showing off this production."

"I hope we don't let you down then!" I say half jokingly, while my brain whirs. Mr. Thomas is gay. That was what he said, wasn't it? Lewis is definitely a man's name. He definitely said "he." I suppose, well, why shouldn't he be gay?

"I'm sure you won't." He looks at his watch, and then up at Grace as she walks across the hall to join us. "There's someone else I need to have a word with before the end of break. Anyway, don't you two need to be off to your next lesson—doing equations or learning historical dates or some such activity that can't be nearly as exciting as English or drama with me?"

As Grace and I leave the hall, she nudges me, "So what was all that chat with Mr. Thomas? It looked serious. I didn't think I could interrupt!"

"Nothing much," I say. "I think he just came out to me, that's all."

"What?" says Grace. "Really? He's gay?" She shakes her head and is quiet for a moment. "Well," she says brightly. "I suppose if he's not going to marry you—or me—and both of those options have always seemed a bit unlikely— then he might as well be gay."

Chapter Thirty-Three

Mom's voice drifts up the stairs. I'm in my bedroom, finishing getting ready to go. She's singing the first line from one of my favourite songs from the show, "Luck Be a Lady," Sam's big number. It's all about luck not deserting you when you need it most—and it's never felt more appropriate.

Then I hear Dee's voice joining in with the second line, before they both sing the chorus together.

I have to admit, despite all the stress and the arguments of the last school year, there's something lighter about Dad now. Mom, too. Like they were holding onto something large and heavy, and they've now realized that they can let go.

"Here you are, Izzy," says Mom, as I come down the

stairs. She doesn't need to say anything else. She's looking so proud that it makes me blush.

Luckily the phone rings and breaks the moment before I go totally beet red. "I'll get it," says Dee, disappearing into the living room.

To my surprise, Vicky is sitting at the kitchen table with a cup of tea. I've been so wrapped up in nerves and excitement that I didn't even hear her come in.

She stands up and hands me a bunch of flowers. I don't know their names, but the colors are beautiful. "These are for afterward really," she says with a smile, "but I thought we should put them in some water now."

"Are you coming then?" I ask, as she pulls me into a hug.

"Wouldn't miss it for the world. If that's okay, of course. . . ."

"That was Grace's mom," interrupts Dee, sticking her head around the kitchen door. "They're still having trouble with their car. So we've made a plan—Vicky's going to take Mom, Megan, and Jamie. Izzy and I will pick up Grace and her mom in our car on the way. Is that okay, Vicky?"

"Suits me," says Vicky. "As long as Kath tells me where we're going. And as long as Jamie holds my hand. I don't think I've been inside a school for more than thirty years, and I'm a little bit nervous." She shudders. It's a joke, I know that, but there's a slight edge to Vicky's normally confident voice.

"Let's get going then, Izzy," says Dee. "Are you ready?"

Dee and I leave first; Mom's still making Jamie wash felt-tip pen off his face. It looks like he and Vicky have had one of their drawing sessions, but not all of the pen made it onto the paper. She's given in on the Spider-Man outfit though—Jamie's still in full superhero mode.

We're almost out of the door when Megan's voice calls me back. I've hardly seen her today. She's been up in her room getting ready since I got home. She's smiling a little nervously as she presses something into my hand. It has the same rough yet smooth feel of her artwork, but is much, much smaller. I open my fingers and there, in red with bold black capitals, is a message written on a papier-mâché disc. It simply says, *GOOD LUCK*. I don't have the right words to say how amazing her artwork is, or how proud I am of her being my sister, or even to say thank you for what she's just given me. So instead I hug her, long and tight. We stand together on the doorstep until Dee beeps her horn and Mom shouts from inside that we're letting all the warm air out.

Dee drives at top speed over to Grace's house, then

waits in the car outside while I dart up the steps to ring the doorbell. After several rings, Grace bounces out, full of apologies for keeping us waiting. At least I don't have to throw gravel at her window to get her to come out. She's followed more slowly by Mrs. Okafor in what must be her best outfit.

"I still don't think my mom knows what it's about," whispers Grace. "I haven't told her it's all about gambling. . . ."

"Or singing and dancing in dodgy clubs . . ." I add.

"Or about the bit when Sarah gets really drunk!"

"At least that's me not you," I reply.

"True. Do you think she'll like it?" Grace looks genuinely worried. It really matters to her what her mom thinks.

"'Course, she will," I say, squeezing her hand. "*You're* in it. She'll *love* it."

Grace and I squish into the back seat. I can hardly believe it was only this morning that we sat here eating breakfast on the way back from the studio. Although, come to think of it, the car does still smell like bacon and the wrappers are all over the floor.

The lights are blazing at school as Dee pulls in to park. As we hop out, another car pulls up alongside ours. Sam opens the door. I can hear him reassuring his parents that they *are* in the right place, and it *is* the right night and *of course* it's okay to park here.

We're so pleased to see him—especially Grace—that we hardly stop and say goodbye to our parents before the three of us are sprinting across the parking lot toward the lighted hall doors. The stage is ready, the empty seats are set out in rows, the costumes and makeup are waiting.

Behind us there's a loud, insistent beeping and we turn back to see what's going on. The rain's stopped and it's a clear, crisp night. The sound carries a long way.

It's Dee beeping the horn, while Sam's mom flashes the headlights on their car.

"Good luck and God bless," shouts Grace's mom, jumping up and down and waving frantically, now that she knows they've caught our attention.

"Break a leg!" yells Dee, blowing us kisses.

Even Sam's mom and dad join in, chanting and waving their scarves in the air like they're at a football game.

Other cars are parking now, and everyone's stopped to look at our parents making a show of themselves.

"Parents, eh?" says Sam, looking at Grace and at me. Despite the shame of it, we all have enormous grins on our faces. He shrugs helplessly. "How embarrassing can you get?" And in we go.

Chapter Thirty-Four

The curtain has gone down for the interval, but the applause is still ringing in my ears. People liked it, I tell myself, amazed, they really did. When I first got onstage, with the house lights down and the stage lights up, I couldn't see anyone in the audience. But I could feel them—shuffling, sighing, breathing, waiting—as I drew breath for my first line.

And then it went in a flash. We sang, we danced. Lucas and Grace got laughs—mostly in the right places. Sam and I remembered all our lines, and I didn't crash into him even once. Now, suddenly, we're halfway through.

"It's nearly over," I whisper to Grace, grabbing her hand as we come offstage.

"Not really, there's still tomorrow and Saturday and all

the rest of tonight. And then there's end of the school year and Christmas and next year."

"I suppose," I murmur. But it's still sad to think that in a couple of days, normal life will start again.

The drama studio is full of people shrieking, shouting, getting in and out of costumes, falling over each other, searching for their bags and checking their phones.

"Ten minutes!" calls Mr. Thomas. "You need to be back in your places, costumes ready, in ten minutes."

I'm desperate for the bathroom. I pick my way through the crowds of people and out of the studio. The door closes behind me and it's suddenly quiet. I breathe deeply and run cold water over my hands at the sink. When I look up, I see Sarah Brown in the mirror. I crack her a smile—and she smiles back.

It's so quiet that I start to worry—perhaps everyone's back in their seats already. Maybe the second half is about to start and I'm going to miss my cue. Maybe—I dash out of the door—and bump straight into Lucas. Just Lucas, no Charlie or Amir, he's by himself. So am I.

He drops the script he's carrying and paper cascades everywhere. We get down on our knees to gather up the sheets.

"Sorry," we both say at the same time. I look up at him.

What's this, Lucas saying sorry? What's that about? Normally he'd just grunt and walk away or find a way to give you an extra push. I look closer. Is he even blushing? I realize that I'm not really sorry at all for bumping into him, even if it was an accident. In fact, I kind of wish I'd done it on purpose.

"Why did you tell everyone about my dad?" I challenge him, trying to catch his eye, but he looks away, embarrassed.

"Dunno," he mutters.

"Come on," I say. "That's not good enough. I deserve to know."

He's still shuffling papers, not looking at me. "Thought it would be funny," he says at last.

"And was it? Was it funny? To make fun of me? To make fun of someone you don't even know, about something you don't even understand?" I'm standing up now, hands on hips, while Lucas stumbles to his feet. My voice is steady and calm, not shrill. It's ringing through the empty corridor, and I don't care who hears.

"I'm sorry, Izzy."

"Oh, really?"

"Yes. Like, it *was* funny, at first. But then, well, doing this play with you has been so good, and Mr. Thomas said . . . and I, well . . . I shouldn't have said all that stuff."

"Mr. Thomas? What's he got to do with it?"

"Oh, he gave me a bit of a warning today, that's all."

I hate being told off. It makes me want to curl into a ball and cry. But I thought Lucas didn't really mind. After all, it happens to him all the time, but maybe, deep down, he does. He looks so small all of a sudden, not scary at all, standing there in his costume, like a kid in a suit pretending to be a grown-up, which of course is exactly what he is. I'm not ready to say anything back like, *It's okay*, or *I forgive you*. I'm still too angry. But right now I don't want to make him feel any worse than he already does.

"How come you've still got your script?" I ask. "You got all your lines okay in the first half."

"Just checking. Don't want to mess it up." We smile nervously at each other.

Only now do I wonder where Grace is. She'd have been amazed to have seen me. A few weeks ago, I would have been amazed, too. But now, I don't know, it feels right, like there's a new Isabel Palmer, one who's not afraid to stand up for herself. I don't *need* Grace, but I still want to tell her all about this strange conversation with Lucas. I haven't seen her—or Sam—since just after we got offstage.

"Time!" calls Mr. Thomas, sticking his head out of the drama-studio door. "Where are my stars? Isabel, Lucas, come on, the second half's about to start!"

The Ending

You still can't convince me that our town is an exciting place to live. Even after everything that happened.

It's still a small town surrounded by nothing much, with hardly anything to do or see or talk about.

In the end, *Guys and Dolls* was amazing, with only a few missed lines and less-than-ideal scene changes. And by closing night, it was pretty much perfect.

Despite everyone telling Lucas how great he was as Nathan Detroit—and he really was in the end—he didn't get bigheaded about it. Big surprise. I don't know what kind of warning Mr. Thomas gave him, but it seems to have worked. He can even be quite nice these days—well, sometimes.

Megan didn't win the art prize, but she didn't seem to

mind. All her research inspired her to become an activist. She's still angry all the time, but about big issues like racism and the arms trade and transphobia, rather than about me going in her room without asking or Mom daring to speak to her before breakfast, so I guess this is better.

Some changes aren't so good. Mr. Thomas is leaving next year. He and Lewis are moving back to Scotland. I'm trying not to think about it. He says we're the best class he's ever had and he's really going to miss us.

Dee's started her hormones. She says it's like being a teenager again. I can't tell if she thinks that's good or bad. We're all getting used to the way things are now and saying "she" is starting to feel natural, not something I always have to think about getting right. Apparently a few people at *Guys and Dolls* gave Dee funny looks, but Megan stared them down. Apart from that, most of them didn't even care.

Sam's dad and Dee go out for a drink every so often. I don't know what they talk about. Whatever it is, I don't think they're talking about us. Grace's mom pops by our house more often now, too, usually with a homemade cake to share, and stops for a cup of tea with Mom.

And me and Grace? Well, I worried that once Grace and Sam became an item, I'd get frozen out. But so far it's

260

okay. Sam's properly my friend now, too. Mr. Thomas has even started calling us the Three Musketeers. And weirdly, actually going out with Sam has stopped Grace going on and on about him all the time. The three of us are going to audition for the summer all-school production together and see if we get lucky again.

Something *did* happen in Littlehaven. And, at first, I wished it hadn't. I thought it was a disaster. I thought I'd lose my dad and then I thought I'd lose my best friend. But I didn't lose either of them, and I gained so much more. Now things are back to boring, everyday normality. Like nothing ever happened here. But I know that it did.

Hello!

Thank you for choosing *Nothing Ever Happens Here*. I really hope you have enjoyed reading Izzy's story.

Your family may be like Izzy's, or it may not, but there's probably something about it that's unique and makes it stand out from other people's. These differences can be embarrassing or scary. They can make you feel totally alone, like you're the only person in the world having this experience. But they can also open you up to new friendships and new ways of seeing the world. They can help you become a kinder or braver person. They can be something to celebrate.

Izzy and her family go through some big changes together, and sometimes change can be stressful or upsetting. At times like these, it can help to talk to someone you trust; a parent, teacher, sibling or friend. On the next

page there's also some details of organizations that you may find useful if you are facing some of the changes experienced by Izzy in this book.

I know lots of families like Izzy's, with parents who are lesbian, gay, bi, or trans (LGBT). After all, my own children have two moms! But I hardly ever see families like these in the books I read. This is partly why I wrote *Nothing Ever Happens Here*—to show that these families exist, too. LGBT people are not strange people "out there somewhere," they are parents, friends, colleagues, and people everyone knows—just like Dee and some of the other characters in this book.

But the main reason that I wrote *Nothing Ever Happens Here* was because I had an idea for a story—and I had to write it so that I could see what would happen next! I hope you liked it.

If you have been affected by some of the issues raised in this book, the following organizations can help or provide further information:

Gay & Lesbian Alliance Against Defamation (GLAAD)

Transgender Resources

https://www.glaad.org/transgender/resources

National Center for Transgender Equality

https://transequality.org/additional-help

The Trevor Project

Trans + Gender Identity

https://www.thetrevorproject.org/trvr_support_center/trans-gender-identity/

Straight for Equality

Trans Ally Resources

https://www.straightforequality.org/transresources

History of the Transgender Pride Flag

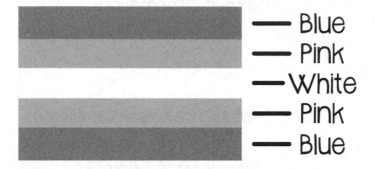

— Blue
— Pink
— White
— Pink
— Blue

The Transgender Pride Flag was created in 1999 by Monica Helms, a transgender woman, activist, author, and US Navy veteran. It consists of five horizontal stripes and three colors. Two outer light blue stripes are representative for boys, two light pink stripes for girls, and a white center stripe for those who are transitioning, intersex, or who have a neutral or an undefined gender. The flag first flew in a Pride parade in Phoenix, Arizona, in 2000 by Helms. If you look at the cover of this book, you will see the colors of the Transgender Pride Flag have been used as an added tool to help tell this story.

To learn more about Monica Helms, visit this website:

http://transveteran.org/board-item/monica-helms/

Acknowledgments

There are a few people I'd like to say thank you to.

First of all—you. There's thousands of fantastic children's books out there, and you chose to read this one. I hope Izzy and her family's story stays with you for a long time. Thank you for reading.

I am someone who is cis (not trans), writing about trans people's lives in this book. That is a perilous thing to do, especially at a time when trans people are often portrayed as oddities or threats. I have tried my hardest to tell this story with respect and realism, and the extent to which I have succeeded is thanks to trans readers and friends, some of whom are mentioned below. Thank you so much. Any mistakes I have made are, of course, all my own.

All the families with lesbian, gay, bi, or trans (LGBT) parents who shared their stories with me for the parenting guide, *Pride and Joy,* which I co-wrote a few years ago. You are the inspiration behind *Nothing Ever Happens Here.* A special thank you to Jess and Justine who not only shared their stories, but also kindly read the first draft and offered comments and encouragement.

Susie, for being one of the first to read *Nothing Ever Happens*

Here. Her incisive, detailed, and thoughtful comments made the book so, so much better and I am really grateful. I look forward to reading her book one day....

Christine and Jay who read the manuscript and made sure I treated the subject matter well. Their opinions really mattered to me and the responses from both Christine and Jay to *Nothing Ever Happens Here* gave me great joy (and even made me cry!).

My former colleagues in the editorial team at CAFOD, working alongside you all has made me a better writer.

My colleagues at Stonewall. Every day I am inspired by the work you do to drive forward LGBT equality and help people "get over it."

Chloe, my agent, who always championed *Nothing Ever Happens Here* and believed in the story I was trying to tell.

Stephanie, my editor, and all the team at Usborne for their encouragement, great ideas, and for guiding me through the publishing process with kindness and creativity.

My mom (always my biggest cheerleader!).

My family—my partner, Rachel, and my children, Esther and Miriam (not forgetting the rabbits Caramel and Cookie)—for your support, editorial comments, and all-around wonderfulness.